Praise for Dead

"Stella Oni brings a welcome new voice and an engagingly fresh perspective in her superbly executed debut crime novel, *Deadly Sacrifice*. A totally absorbing read."

—Jacob Ross, author of *Black Rain Falling*
and *The Bone Readers*

"An audacious début novel..."

—Nii Ayikwei Parkes, author of *Tail of the Blue Bird*

"*Deadly Sacrifice* is a gripping read. It's a foray into the gritty underbelly of human trafficking and London's more deprived communities, where immigration and social stratification are interlinked in 21st-century Britain. A chilling tale, powered by a likeable Nigerian-British heroine."

—Winnie M Li, author of *Dark Chapter*

"A gripping debut that keeps you turning the pages. A brilliant debut from Stella Oni."

—Leye Adenle, author of *When Trouble Starts* and
Easy Motion Tourist

"An excellent page-turner that delves into a difficult subject. Wealth and poverty, hope and loss, the divine and the squalid jostle among this novel's pages, the whole navigated and mediated by doughty, fledgling detective, DC Toks Ade. She is a refreshing addition to British crime fiction, and I hope to see much more of her."

—Peter Kalu, author of *Yard Dogs*

DEADLY SACRIFICE

Stella Oni

JACARANDA

TWENTY in 2020
Black Writers, British Voices

This edition first published in Great Britain 2020
Jacaranda Books Art Music Ltd
27 Old Gloucester Street,
London WC1N 3AX
www.jacarandabooksartmusic.co.uk

Copyright © Stella Oni 2020

The right of Stella Oni to be identified as the author of this work
has been asserted in accordance with the Copyright, Designs and
Patents Act 1988.

All rights reserved. No part of this publication may be reproduced,
stored in a retrieval system, distributed, or transmitted in any form
or by any means, including photocopying, recording, or other elec-
tronic or mechanical methods, without the prior written permission of the copyright owners and the publisher.

A CIP catalogue record for this book is available from the British
Library

ISBN: 9781913090241
eISBN: 9781913090449

Cover Design: Jeremy Hopes
Typeset by: Kamillah Brandes

Printed and bound by CPI Group (UK) Ltd, Croydon CR0 4YY

For Daddy,
RIP

Deuteronomy 32:17
They sacrificed to demons, not to God,
To gods they did not know,
To new gods, new arrivals
That your fathers did not fear

One

When Detective Sergeant Philip Dean and Detective Constable Toks Ade stepped out of the warmth of their car into the chilly embrace of a winter day, a disturbing, gruesome find was the last thing on their mind. With the wind whipping at her neck, sharp as razor blades, DC Toks wished she had remembered to bring her woolly scarf.

'Let's hope we're not chasing shadows,' said Philip Dean.

'Shadows?' she asked, glancing sideways at him. He was a tall man with thinning brown hair, pale skin and a downcast expression. She had come under his wing as a trainee detective at the Stamford CID unit in East London when her appointed supervisor became ill.

'Nothing. Don't worry about it,' he muttered.

They were at Cedar Estate, a sprawling, human cauldron of a place, to visit a Mrs Bello, whose 9-year-old grand-daughter had gone missing 2 days before. Toks was here to act as a *Yoruba* interpreter. The team that came to interview Mrs Bello had complained they could not understand her or she could not understand them, who knows. This would be her first proper case on the unit as a detective. She was relieved to be out of police uniform after 10 years.

'Yoruba,' Philip Dean changed the subject. 'I'm trying to learn. Do you know any Igbo or Hausa?'

'No. Just Yoruba.' She did not let her surprise show at his knowledge of the 3 main Nigerian languages. She continued to scan the area as she spoke. Mrs Bello's flat was in one of the many tower blocks on the estate. She heard some laughter and saw that on the other side of the path were low walls surrounding a wide, raised concrete platform that acted as a bridge and entry to four tower blocks. In what she thought might be Mrs Bello's block, she eyed a communal bin of over-flowing discarded furniture—mattresses with foamy entrails, chairs with missing arms, a gas cooker with a blackened heart. She saw a few boys joyfully kicking a football through puddles of yesterday's dirty rain water. As they approached, Toks saw that the boys had stopped and were crouched over something on the ground. She suddenly felt a tingling in her belly from her uniformed days.

'You okay there, boys?' she called out.

They jumped back and turned pale, shocked faces to the detectives. A boy with spiky blonde hair pointed a shaky finger to the ground.

'A hand! Whisky found a hand!'

He seemed to wake up the rest as they tried to all talk at once. Toks turned to a pimply boy of about 14 who seemed to be the oldest. He said his name was Tommy. He was desperately trying to contain a Yorkshire Terrier that was whipping itself against its leash, adding its frenzied barking to the confusion.

'Whisky brang it to me,' he said. 'He dropped it at my feet. I thought it was a stick... I...' his voice broke.

Philip Dean waved his hand. 'Boys, move back and let's see.'

With an eye kept on the boys, Toks watched him take a long look at the thing on the ground before turning to her with a grimace. 'Welcome to East London CID, Detective Ade.' He slid his hand into his faded fisherman's jacket and brought out his phone.

Toks stared at the tiny human hand, severed at the wrist, little fingers swollen and split like a bunch of rotting bananas. There was a stench of gone off meat. Could it be the missing girl? She dismissed it. That was only 2 days ago.

She turned back to the boys, thankful that none had tried to leave.

'Boys, I am Detective Ade and this is Detective Dean. We are the police.'

'You're not wearing uniforms. Are you undercover?' asked the little boy with the spiky hair.

Toks overheard snippets of Philip Dean's conversation as she answered the boy.

'Cedar Estate,' he said, his eyes on their find. Once he finished the call, he turned to the boys. 'Detective Ade here will take your names and addresses and we will call your parents.' He turned to Toks. 'I'm going to get some tape to cordon off this area for the scene of crime officers.'

With the image of the hand still imprinted in her mind, she moved the children to the side. There were six of them jostling restlessly with varying expressions of awe and shock on their faces. They looked dirty and unkempt in their clothing, except for the spiky haired boy. He was smart in his designer trainers and jogging suit. It was hard to imagine that any of these boys had been playing and jumping less than 5 minutes before. She picked Tommy, the pimply boy. The terrier had now quietened its barking to low growls.

'Can you tell me what happened with your dog?'

'Whisky's not my dog. She's Sarah's dog. That's our neighbour.' He shuffled from one foot to the other.

'That's right, Miss,' one of the other boys said.

The spiky haired boy suddenly started to whimper and then burst into tears. 'Are you going to arrest us, Miss? 'Cos I've got to go.'

'She's not going to arrest us,' said a chubby boy. 'She's going to ask us about what Whisky found. Like on TV.'

Toks had to stop herself from smiling. 'What's your name?' she asked the boy.

'Andrew Jones, Miss. 36 Forest House.' He pointed to the block on the right.

Conscious of their widened eyes on Philip, who was cordoning off the area with red crime scene tape, she quickly took their details. 'I also need to take your phones,' she said, knowing that pictures of the find would be nestling in some of the phones, ready to be zapped into Instagram and Snapchat.

'Miss, we need our phones!' said Spiky boy.

'I promise we will return them, but I need to speak to your parents before you go.'

She held her hand out and with low mutterings and grumbles they handed her their phones.

'Right,' she turned to little spiky hair. 'Shall we start with you?'

Toks made the calls one at a time and spoke to parents and carers, conscious of Philip's movements. Some sounded anxious and others indifferent. She made careful note before turning to the boys.

'You can go now. Your families are expecting you.'

As if in silent agreement, they turned and ran. Soon each disappeared into a block. The now empty space held the ghost of their previous laughter. Toks and Philip heard sirens and within minutes police cars started to converge around them. The place had started to swarm with curious occupants of the tower blocks and uniformed officers were trying to push them back. SOCO, the Scene of Crime Officers arrived in their van and Toks walked closely behind Philip as he showed them the find.

'The dog was digging the grass in that corner...' he said. Her eyes followed his finger, pointing to a small bushy clump clinging to the wall of the plateau, '...and brought what it's owner thought was a stick...'

She saw that SOCO were not wasting any time as they set to work videoing and photographing the scene. They began to fan out and started the slow task of combing the area. She shivered. Who was this child? It was a Black child, that much she could see. Were there more body parts to discover? A mist of rain started and she prayed it away under her breath. It was enough that it had rained yesterday with some vital evidence now perhaps washed away. They didn't need more.

What seemed to be hours later, Detective Chief Inspector Stephen Jackson arrived, followed by Dr Olive Rothman, the home office pathologist. Toks knew her by sight as she had attended a few of her crime scenes when she was a uniform. Dr Rothman had a smooth oval face and glossy dark hair that was pulled back in a chignon this evening. Her delicate build was sheathed in a well cut, black wool coat. Toks immediately felt like an elephant beside a ballerina.

'Hello, what have we got here?' Dr Rothman said in a deep melodious voice that was hard to equate with her petite build. She put down a large black bag. 'It had better be good, Philip. That was a great concert you pulled me out of.' She gave him a tight smile before walking straight to the cordoned off area. She fluidly bent down and used a gloved hand to carefully turn the hand palm up. Toks heard her swift intake of breath. She rummaged in her bag until Toks saw her bring out a magnifying glass. Philip had also crouched down beside her. They began a muttered conversation. DCI Jackson, who had been unusually quiet, looked at them with an irritated expression. He always reminded Toks of a big gruff bear. 'Anything we need to know?' he growled. Rothman looked up as Philip stood, his face impassive.

'What is it, Olive?' asked Jackson.

She pressed her lips together and Toks tensed. 'The palm

is scarred, like it was pressed on some hot surface,' she said. 'Possibly an electric hob.'

Toks found it difficult to distinguish a burn on the rotted palm.

Jackson frowned and puffed out his jowly, red-veined cheeks. 'Some kind of abuse?'

'I don't know,' the pathologist answered. 'I'll try and find out more once I get it to the lab. We are looking at a rot that would have started a week or more ago. I suggest you start looking for a body.' She straightened. 'I wish you luck with this one, guys. I hope we haven't got another Alpha on our hands.'

Toks felt a tremor go through her body. *The torso in the Thames. But that was 13 or 14 years ago! Then again, his killers were never found.*

Two

The crowd around the crime scene continued to increase, people pushing forward to see what was happening within the taped area. Toks saw Philip quietly moving around and snapping pictures of the crowd with his phone. No-one took any notice of him. The uniformed officers worked to push the crowd back, but suddenly there was a commotion, and an elderly Black woman burst through the tape before two of the officers leapt forward to hold her back. Short, round and wearing a brightly printed African headscarf, she struggled against the officer as her eyes rolled back. Toks tried to listen to her rants through the scuffle.

'Venus. You have found my child. Venus…'

It was the grandmother they were meant to interview! Philip went to the woman.

'Mrs Bello, it's not Venus. You need to allow the officers to take you home,' he said.

She stopped and seemed to slump into the strong arms of Red John, a brawny officer with bright red hair. He laid her on the floor, listened to her breathing and looked up.

'She's fine. I think she just fainted. We should call an ambulance all the same.'

'I've done that,' said Philip. 'Toks, I'd like you to go with her and do the questions as soon as she comes round.'

Toks nodded. It was easier than watching the SOCO searching the area for a dead child. The ambulance arrived and Mrs Bello, who had by now woken up, started protesting loudly as the paramedics began their checks on her.

'There's nothing wrong. Leave me o. My grandson is at home. You have said this is not my granddaughter.' She struggled to sit up and, after a few attempts, succeeded. She waved the paramedics away. Toks looked at Philip. He nodded. She knew what he wanted.

'Ma,' Toks said, addressing her as a Yoruba would address an elderly woman. 'I will escort you back home.'

***

At the huge steel door that barred entry to her block, Mrs Bello brought out a fob to tap against the numbered keypad. Before she could pull the heavy door, it opened and an elderly Chinese man came out with a Yorkshire Terrier that looked like Whisky's cousin. The little dog went to squat in a miserable tuft of grass near the bins and started ejecting brown, stringy turds. The old man ignored it and peered at them with rheumy eyes.

'Ah,' he said in a deep voice. 'Have you found child? I see lot police?'

'Mr Chan. Thank you. I don't know what they have found, but it is not my granddaughter.'

'Ah…good…good,' his eyes moved to Toks. 'You will find her. Be faithful.'

'Thank you,' Mrs Bello answered, ushering Toks through the door.

They entered a lobby with walls covered in large, illegible graffiti and waited for the lift which arrived with a ping.

'Come,' she said to Toks as she briskly entered the urine-sodden lift. She pressed her floor number and within a few minutes of ammonia laden air, they were on Floor 21. Toks almost ran out. The smell brought back memories of her days in a council flat like this. An old woman, with thin, sparse hair, was mopping the tiled floor with a filthy looking mop. She stopped and glared at them with protruding, red-rimmed eyes. After muttering under her breath, she continued her task. Mrs Bello thrust her keys into her door and looked over her shoulder.

'See you later, Maisie,' she said. The old woman did not look up.

Mrs Bello shrugged and opened the door. 'Come in, my daughter.'

Toks entered and the woman shut the door. 'Maisie has good days and bad. I think they should home her. I told those carers but nobody will listen.'

Tok's first impression of the flat was obscured by the smell that hit her nostrils. She started to cough. Mrs Bello was cooking pepper soup and she knew it had more than enough of the scorching, hot scotch bonnet peppers so well loved by Nigerians. She followed Mrs Bello down a short hallway into a small, bright blue room crammed with three overstuffed chairs. The only other piece of furniture was a heavy brown cabinet set against the wall. It had a dirty, dusty look. Two large windows carved into the wall opposite provided a view from a sheer 21 floor drop. Family photos covered a section of another wall. Mrs Bello seemed to suddenly notice Tok's discomfort and clasped her hands to her ample chest.

'Aah! The pepper soup. I'm sorry o. It's for my grandson. He has a bad cold.' She moved to the windows and pushed them open. 'Sorry, sorry. Let me switch the cooker off.' Toks snuffled silently. As soon as Mrs Bello left, she walked to the wall of photographs. There was a striking one of two children in school uniform—a girl of about 9, hair in pigtails, tiny face, large dark eyes, full lips, and skin light enough to possibly be mixed-race. It was one of those standard photographs taken in schools. She had had enough of those with Bode, her son. The little girl's eyes held a maturity and knowing look beyond her years. The boy was the image of the girl, except for the fact that he had short curly hair, twinkling dark eyes, and full lips, deliberately pinched together, as if he was bursting to play some mischief. The dark blue pullover that both of them wore had a logo and the school's name—Tallis Primary School. Toks was turning to check the other pictures when she heard a door slam. She took a seat.

'Sorry to keep you waiting. Have you more questions? These white police officers, they were looking at me as if I was speaking a foreign language. Is it not this English language that we all speak? I have told them everything. I have told the social care people everything eh? What more?'

Toks brought out her notebook. 'Ma, sorry that it looks like we ask the same questions, but sometimes we catch little details in your answers. That is why I'm here today.'

She smelt the pepper soup spices on Mrs Bello as the woman moved closer to her. Her nose started tingling again.

'What is going on downstairs? What did they find?' she asked in a whisper.

'Ma, not much. About Venus…' Toks said in Yoruba. 'You said she was going out to play…'

'My daughter. I was surprised to hear you speak earlier. You have the look of the east of Nigeria. Are you sure you're full Yoruba?'

'Yes, I am, Ma,' said Toks.

'I will try to answer again,' she said. 'Venus came back from school, had her lunch and said she was going out to play with her friend, Teresa.'

'What time did she leave?'

'About 4. When I called Teresa's house at 6 o'clock, her mum said they never saw Venus. That got me very worried. I called 'round her other friends in the area and they say they did not see her.' Tears trickled down her cheeks.

'Where's your grandson?'

'He's resting,' she said, quickly, her eyes sliding away from Toks as she spoke.

'Could I speak to him briefly?'

'What do you want to speak to him for?' She threw her hands up in the air. 'He's not the one that is missing. He's not the one you should be looking for.'

Toks became more polite. 'Ma, I really need to speak to him. Whatever information he can give us will help. They are twins?'

Mrs Bello looked resigned. 'Yes, they are. I will call him.' She left the room again.

Toks thought about all the gaps that Philip would need to fill in, in order for them to understand this case properly. Her anxiety ratcheted up as she realised that this girl had been missing for 48 hours. The trail was growing cold. She looked at the picture and said a quiet prayer for her. Philip also said that the children were under care. She needed to know why. Mrs Bello appeared with a little figure trailing behind her.

'Greet our visitor, Joseph. This nice woman is police. Her name is Aunty Toks.'

'Hello, Joseph,' Toks greeted him with a smile. He looked smaller than his 9 years.

'Hello,' he replied. She saw the cheeky face in the picture come to life. 'Are you going to find Venus?'

'We hope to find her but I need to ask you some questions. Do you know where your sister went from here?'

'She said she was going to see Triz.'

'Is Teresa called Triz?' she asked and he nodded.

'Did she say she would be going anywhere else from Triz's?'

'No. She wanted to play with Triz's karaoke and said I wasn't invited. I don't like boy bands anyway. I like wrestling and games. Grandma is going to buy me a PlayStation for Christmas.'

'PlayStation is expensive. This boy!' said Mrs Bello. 'Come. You need to eat some pepper soup.' Before Toks could open her mouth again, the woman pulled him by his hand. 'He has to eat and he has a bad cold.'

The boy scowled. 'Grandma!' Mrs Bello pushed him out of the room.

Toks went back to her study of the pictures on the wall. There was one of Mrs Bello looking young and elegant in a blouse and long skirt made out of Swiss lace material favoured by Nigerians for celebrations. She ran her eyes over the wall to see if she could see anything resembling the children's parents, but realised they were all of Mrs Bello or the children.

'I like to put our pictures on the wall.' She hadn't noticed when she came back in. 'I am the only one these children have. My daughter took drugs till she ended up in care. Their father could be anywhere in the world. Men of these days! That is my life now, my daughter.'

'Sorry, Ma. We will check everything. It will help us if you prepare a list of people that Venus knows – friends and family.'

She stood looking at Toks with a frown. 'I will make the list.'

'Thank you, Ma.' Toks turned to go but Mrs Bello jumped in front of her and headed for the front door. She had to follow her round, curved back. The pepper soup odour had grown faint. The woman turned several locks before the door swung open.

'Bye, my daughter. I hope you will bring us good news.' She shut the door and Toks heard the locks and bolts turning. There was no sign of the old lady, Maisie. She got back to see that SOCO had dug several holes around the area of the find and were bent over the grounds, searching. She almost ran to where Philip stood with Jackson and Rothman. They looked grave and discouraged.

Philip nodded to her and came to her side.

He watched her approach with an inscrutable expression.

'Any progress?' she asked.

'Not really. It may take a while to scour the area. How did it go? Sorry. Left you to it.'

'No bother,' she said, 'although, I think she's a bit strange.'

'Yes. She was a bit agitated with the uniforms. I suppose that's where you come in. Speaking Yoruba to her might calm her down a bit. Did you get anything?'

'Her grandson, Joseph, said the same thing as the grand-mother... she was meant to meet her friend Teresa. I think we should dig a little bit. It's worth looking back and checking the list of their mother's old boyfriends. Venus could also have run away. As you said, social services were planning to remove her from her grandmother for difficult and challenging behaviour. We'll need to talk to Teresa.'

'She's in that block, 3rd floor.' He pointed to a block identical to Mrs Bello's. 'The uniforms went there yesterday and got a bad reception. DC Foster said the mother wouldn't allow them to meet the girl.'

***

That evening, tired and hungry, Toks turned her grey Toyota into the dark street of her house in Dagenham and imagined she was already in the bath having a long soak. It had been a hard day. She could not believe that her first job out of uniform was a child butcher. She remembered The Torso in the Thames, all those years ago. They never found the rest of his body. Today, news vans had jammed the area as they were leaving and Toks knew she wouldn't be the only one making the Alpha connection. She parked in front of her semi-detached house and gazed at it proudly. The street was quiet at this time. Some windows shone with muted light and others with the flickering TV sets. The windows of the Patels across the street were dark. The old couple usually turned in early. Mr Patel, a retired accountant, had told her he might put his house on the market and move back to India. His three children were grown and married with their own kids.

She stood amazed that this house she had bought at auction for £50,000 years ago was now worth so much. She thanked her father, a retired architect, who had spotted it's potential on a visit from Nigeria and urged her to move out of her council flat and buy her own place. He had been one of the best in his days. Their family home, that he had built, was so aesthetically stunning that people had come from all over the country just to look at it.

Once inside her house, Toks exhaled in relief and slid off her shoes at the entrance. She closed her eyes as her feet sank into deep cream carpet. She loved the feeling of softness and had refused the more fashionable wooden flooring.

'Hiya, I'm home,' she called out to Bode.

He came out of the sitting room where she could hear the blare of rap slightly echoing.

'Hello, Mum.' Toks smiled at the deep voice.

She was tall, but at 15, Bode was already towering over her. It amazed her how much he looked like Femi with his light, faintly freckled skin. He was quite lanky, but Toks knew he would fill out like his dad. She remembered how Femi had come back a few years before to try and see his son, begging her for forgiveness. Then, she had been unbending in her feelings towards him, but now Bode was becoming a man and she had no substitute father for him.

'How is school?' she asked.

'Same old, same old,' he muttered.

'You sure things are ok?' She gave him a quick hug.

'*Yes*, mum,' he rolled his eyes then met hers. She held his gaze for a moment and his eyes dropped. That was their game. He found it hard to look her in the eyes and lie.

'I'm fine Mum, honestly.'

He was an intelligent boy—getting into grammar school had proved that. But she had already had to visit his school more than once this year because he had gotten into fights. She hadn't relished the subsequent conversation on the system designed to put 'troublesome' Black teenage boys in youth detention.

'I hope you can do a spot of mowing tomorrow, young

25

man. That grass will soon be taller than both of us,' she said as she started up the stairs.

'Mum?' She turned. He looked uncomfortable. 'Did you have anything to do with that discovery today? You know… the child's hand? They were talking about it on TV.'

Toks tried not to bring work home, but sometimes she gave him as much as he needed to know.

'Kind of. We don't know what to make of it.'

'They say there was a torso of an African boy found in the Thames, like years ago. Why are people doing this?' He looked angry.

'Is there something I should know, Bode?' Toks asked quietly.

'Just some stupid boys telling me Africans are juju worshippers and scammers.'

'We don't know whether this has any connection with the torso. Don't let the idiots get to you.'

'Alright, Mum.'

She wearily continued up the stairs to draw herself a bath. Submerging herself in achingly hot water, she let the day's troubles swiftly melt away.

Three

Philip Dean watched his twin sister across the small stark room that contained a single bed, a chest of drawers and a sink in the corner. Everything else had been pronounced 'harmful'. Her collar bones protruded sharply and he could see the deep-purple veins beneath her pale skin. He recalled how Emily used to struggle to lose her curvy figure. Her hair hung in thinned oily strands. The manager had told him it was a struggle to get her to wash each day, let alone brush her hair.

'How are you?' he asked.

'Fine.' Her lips were a slash of orange from the lipstick that she had requested he bring the week before.

'I saw it on TV, you know. Knew immediately you were part of it. I felt it,' she said holding his eyes with her crazed ones.

'What did you see on TV?' At her most lucid Emily was ferociously bright, and at her worst she was so violent that the foul words that spewed out of her mouth were enough to make her carers weep.

'The hand that was discovered from that dirty, nasty place.

You go into those stinking houses and it will be one of them. They kill children and eat them.'

Emily had been diagnosed with schizophrenia years before.

'Did you bring my lipstick? I'm sick of this orange.'

She had been a prize-winning headteacher, turning around two inner city schools and taking them to the top of the league table. Her school had competed with the best private schools. It had all happened quickly. No outward sign that anything was wrong. Only that a member of staff had found her naked and trying to jump out from her office window. She had told Philip later that a saintly voice had told her it was for the best. That was the beginning of their misery.

'Yes, I brought it. And some biscuits.' He held up a small supermarket carrier bag. She snatched it off him and spilled the contents onto her narrow bed. Philip looked out of her tiny barred window. He did not look forward to going out into the bleak, windy weather.

She eyeballed him. 'What are you worried about? I can feel *you* in my head.' She started to pull at her sparse hair in agitation.

And sometimes I can feel your madness. He stood up abruptly. 'I had better go.'

She did not even notice him as she continued to say her words in sing song with her back to him.

He gently closed the door behind him.

***

Later, with great relief, Philip stepped into his flat in Stamford Hill, North London. He lived in a large Jewish community and sometimes wished he was religious as he watched his neighbours observe the sabbath and other holidays. It seemed so reassuring, yet he knew he could never believe. To him you live, do what you need to do on this earth, and die. That simple. He took off his coat and brought out the Vindaloo he had bought from the supermarket. He punctured the clear film and placed it in the microwave. He missed Misha, the maid that came to cook and clean for him twice a week. Old Mrs Abraham, his neighbour who sometimes left a cooked meal on his doorstep, had recommended Misha and he had gratefully accepted her. Misha was off for a few days visiting family in Manchester, so it was a microwave and a sink full of dirty mugs for him. He avoided the sink and ground the beans for his strong coffee. Jackson had told him that the murder squad were overwhelmed by the knifings in the capital and were handing the case over to them for now. Toks, new to murder cases, would still be useful for their other missing girl case.

***

Scented candles flickered their warm light over Toks as she sank into her silky foam bath. She almost moaned with pleasure. This was her chillout zone. The place where she also sometimes gossiped with her friend Coretta. She carefully reached for her phone and speed-dialled her.

'Hey,' she said.

'Toks! I was just thinking of you.' Coretta sounded breathless.

Toks knew that tone. 'I'm just catching up on you, girl. But now that you say it, what are you up to?

'Nothing! Do I have to be cooking up something to think of you?'

Toks pictured her friend's wild curly hair that she sometimes tied in a loose ponytail, her tiny face and dark forceful eyes. She didn't believe her. Coretta was a self-confessed obsessive former investigative journalist who now wrote award-winning true crime books.

'You can't fool me, Mrs Davies. How is Richard?' asked Toks, about Coretta's husband.

'He's fine. I have a new investigation,' her friend whispered.

'Brilliant.' Toks knew her voice was cautious. Coretta's investigations were never ordinary and she had made a lot of enemies on the way. It was incredible how her 5 foot nothing friend inspired fear in some circles. Her first work about African female drug mules had taken her to Nigeria where her sister, Melissa, lived. She had upset some big guns and fled, leaving her sister's husband to pacify certain factions.

'What is it this time?' asked Toks.

'Human trafficking,' her friend said quietly.

Coretta's second book had been on Black youths and gun crime. She had discovered that organised crime groups like the Chinese Triads and the Naples Mafia used gangs to send Black youths out on the streets as drug mules. They did not discriminate and usually offered each gang substantial money as long as the job got done. This resulted in sporadic violence ending in knife stabbings and shootouts. One time, Coretta got caught in a crossfire between two rival gangs in a south London council estate and was lucky to escape with her life. She had won her first award with the book.

'Tell me about your case, Toks,' she said.

'Nothing much to tell. We're still searching for the missing girl and now we have this.'

'I hope you get a break soon... Toks?'

'Yes?'

'My investigation...it's connected to that young boy years ago—Alpha. Do you think your find is related?'

Toks fell silent.

'Are you still there?'

She would prefer Coretta's project not to be linked to whatever she was doing. She knew she would really need to be careful with her. Coretta was brilliant at her work. She didn't win prizes for nothing.

'I'm still here.'

'I promise not to tread on your path. It's just how it is.'

'Yes,' said Toks.

'Talk to you later? Don't get too wrinkled in that bath.'

'Talk later,' she said. The phone went dead.

Toks sat up in the bath. Should this be something to tell Philip? She dismissed the thought immediately, but left the bath with a feeling of unease.

***

Toks signed in at the station at 7.00 the next morning and found Philip at his desk looking as if he had spent the night there. He looked weary but had his usual unreadable face. Goodness! Was he born like that?

Without even a hello he said, 'We've got an appointment to see Venus's social worker and later, her mother. SOCO have come up with nothing so far. Door to door is still going on.'

'Have we heard anything from the lab?' she asked.

'Nothing.'

He checked his watch. 'The Superintendent wants to see everyone in 15 minutes.'

She hurried to her desk to catch up on some paperwork.

'Hey Toks, heard you caught a good one yesterday.' A voice said close behind her. It was a stout, balding colleague they nicknamed 'Garlicky' Blackstone for his voracious consumption of raw garlic and the pungent smell in his wake. If only he took a daily shower it might have helped.

'Yep,' Toks said, almost choking from his nearness. 'How are the boys?' He was a father to three-year-old twin boys.

He grinned happily.

'Driving me mad.'

They saw colleagues trooping to the meeting room. 'On your feet, Toks. Let's see what Posh Amos says about body parts and missing children.'

She followed him to the rapidly filling incident room. They sat in grey plastic chairs that faced a huge white screen.

DCI Jackson and Superintendent Amos came in. The Superintendent was a lean man in his late-fifties who had been in the force a long time. He greeted them briskly. Their eyes were fixed on the screen as it lit up at his touch and a magnified version of the severed hand came into view. A ragged, blackish stump showed where it had been chopped off.

He pointed at the screen. 'A child's dismembered hand was found at Cedar estate yesterday,' he began without preamble. 'Black child between the age of 4 and 6 years.' He looked grave. 'Hard to know if it's something like the torso in the Thames or not. I say let's not make any assumptions.

'Hand was chopped off—maybe a machete or cutlass. Good to know as the trail might get cold too quickly. We mustn't miss vital clues. Another worrying and possibly related aspect, is the disappearance of a 9-year-old girl, Venus Bello.' Toks watched as Venus's face came into view.

'She went missing 3 days ago and we have full alert out for her. It was on their way to interviewing her grandmother that Dean and Ade came across this. To distinguish between the two cases we shall call this one Little Eva. We have checked the records of recently released paedos who might live in the area.' His eyes swept their faces. 'Dean, Ade, Katherine, Peter, and a full team will work on this. The murder squad are overwhelmed with knife crimes at the moment so you will report to me as SIO.' His eyes swept from DCI Jackson and Philip.

'We will continue to go house to house and try and sift through the information from the public. Most importantly, don't dismiss anything. The pressure is on for us to solve this and close. DCI?'

DCI Jackson jumped to his feet and took over. 'We know Brian Cody was released from prison just a week ago. He lives on a street 5 minutes from Cedar estate. We're tossing him to DS Dean for questioning.' He looked at Philip.

After the meeting, Philip signalled for Toks to stay. She watched the scowl on Jackson's face as he spoke to him. 'We need speed on this, Philip. Let's show the squad how it's done. This is our chance.'

He looked at Toks as if seeing her for the first time. 'Ok, Ade?'

'Yes, sir,' she said.

He turned to Philip.

'It's probable this child is dead. Can't see them surviving in someone's basement with a chopped hand. You've got to turn every stone. I'm trusting you on this.' Toks noticed a look pass between them.

'We are stretched, remember. We still have the missing girl.'

She watched DCI Jackson's face redden.

'You take what you get,' he said, coldly. 'Besides, you've got Katherine and Pete, and a good team combing everywhere.' He turned and left.

If a face could get even stiffer, Philip's did. 'Let's go.'

Four

As Toks and Philip walked back to the estate, she felt a sense of déjà vu and almost expected to see the boys playing football again and everything else that followed. She eyed the small mounds of earth like anthills that SOCO left behind. Where were the remains of that poor child?

'Let's see if we'll get anywhere with Teresa's mum this time.' Philip's voice brought her back.

'We can only try,' she said.

'I'll leave you to do the questioning then,' he said. She almost believed he was amused. But at what? She was surely not a clown.

She squared her shoulders as they made their way to the block. She pressed 36 on the keypad and heard the intercom ringing. 'Who is it?' It was the voice of a young woman.

'Police,' she said.

'Oh!' The entry door buzzed and Philip pulled the iron door open. The 7th floor was similar to Mrs Bello's, and had the same air of neglect. A flat door opened and a tiny, bony woman holding onto the hand of a young girl of about 9 came out. As she saw Toks, her thin lips turned even thinner. A history of chain smoking lay mapped on her prematurely wrinkled face. The darkening roots of her dyed blonde hair were tied in a severe pony tail that further sharpened her ferret features. She waited as they approached.

'Mrs Jones….'

'Haven't seen the gel. Don't want to have nothing to do with you. Don't know nothing about her.'

'….I am Detective Ade and this is Detective Dean.' Philip nodded and stood to the side. Toks showed the woman her warrant card. 'You look as though you're about to go out—can I have a few minutes?'

The girl by the woman's side, whom Toks took to be Teresa, stood quietly, watching. She noted the way the girl steadily stared at her. The mother turned her back, opened the door of the flat, and shoved her back in.

'Go back inside, Triz,' she said harshly and shut the door. 'The gel did not come 'ere. She and Triz used to have a tutor come around for Maths and English. That's stopped and I don't want her comin near my Triz no more. She's no good for my child. Her so young and messin wit dem druggie boys round the estate. I don't want my child anywhere round 'er and I told 'er so.'

'When was the last time you saw Venus?' Toks asked, ignoring her tirade, although noting the implication that Venus was sexually active at 9 years old.

'In school. When 'er gran came to collect 'er. Couple of days ago. Awright? Got to go. Triz 'n me's got an appointment at the doctors. Triz? You can come out now.'

She unlocked the door and then walked round Toks to press the lift button. Teresa came out and walked to her mother's side. Mrs Jones tapped her foot impatiently as she turned her back to them.

'Do you know of any other friends she would have gone to visit?' asked Toks.

'Tina and Joe.' They all turned in surprise. Teresa looked at her mother defiantly. The woman's face reddened. 'Stagg House. Flat 20. Ta,' she said as her mother dragged her into the open maws of the lift.

'You handled that well. That was more than we got before. Let's go find Joe. It's my turn this time.' He smiled grimly.

***

Flat 20 was on the 2nd floor but they decided to take the lift, which stank strongly of urine with bits of wet floor covered in soggy newspaper. They came out onto a dreary landing. Philip could not see a bell so he rapped on the door. Shouts came from inside, and the door jerked open, filling their senses with the smell of frying chips in rancid oil. A pudgy boy with short brown hair glared at Philip and said, 'What d'yer wan? Jordan's not here.'

'We're here to see you, Joe,' he said.

The boy's eyes widened. 'You're the copper from the day Whisky found the hand.'

'Who's that, Joe?' a shrill voice came from inside.

'It's the police. Says they want to 'ave a word wi' me.'

An attractive young woman of about 20, with bright blue eyes and bow shaped lips, appeared behind him. She looked Philip up and down with hostile eyes. 'Get the fuck away, the both of you!' she said.

Philip raised his warrant card for her to see. 'Can I have a word with your mum?'

'Ma!' she shouted, still looking at Philip. 'The filth want to 'ave a word with yer. Should I send them away? You owe dem nuffin… Ma!' She was suddenly shoved out of the way. 'Ow!' A large woman with tired eyes gazed at him.

"Ow can I 'elp ya?"

He explained about Venus possibly seeing Joe on the day of her disappearance. 'They've already been and talked to 'im. What more do yous all want? My Joe tol' dem what he saw and there's no more to it than that. 'Init Joe?'

He nodded his head hard. 'Yes, Ma. I only saw the thing Whisky picked up.'

'May we come in?' asked Philip.

She reluctantly stood back and let them through a short wide corridor to a small and surprisingly clean front room. A chubby baby sucking on a grimy dummy lay fast asleep on a cot wedged in a corner. The girl who met him at the door flopped onto a chair and folded her arms.

'We know Venus is friends with Joe.'

'She's a slag!'

They all swung round to look at Joe who was sitting in the middle of a sofa with a triumphant look on his face. 'She is.

I saw her and Harry together. Ask Tim. He saw dem as well. They went into that little shed near dem stairs.'

'Is Tim…' Philip looked down at the paper wedged into his notebook filled with the names of the boys Toks took down on the day of the find. 'Tim Buckle?'

'Joe. Why are you chatting to them? Dey got nuffink to give you except grief. Ma, why are you allowing it? They have our Jordan locked away and yet you talk to dem? Bet it's all a load of bollocks.'

He ignored his sister while he chanted out Tim's address which matched what Philip had on his piece of paper. His mum stood resigned as two toddlers, a boy and girl, came into the room and held onto her food spattered skirt.

'I bet it's that old pervy down the road,' said Joe.

'Pervy?' asked Philip.

The boy saw his tense interest. 'Yeah. Dat man with de ponytail. He started coming here again.'

'Do you remember the last time you saw him?' asked Philip.

''Bout 2 weeks ago. He used to come here all the time.'

'Do you know where he lives?'

'Down the road from 'ere. The address is… I know, I know,' he was jumping up and down in excitement. 'It's dat house with dem dwarves in the garden. It's the only house down that road with dem.'

'Thank you, Joe. Thank *you*,' he said to the mum.

''ope I don't see yous here again. I've got enough on me plate as it is,' she said grimly.

'I'm afraid we might still come back,' he said.

Philip checked his watch. It was 11:00. They had an appointment at 12 with Mary Grant, Venus's social worker.

Toks took several gulps of fresh air once they got outside. There was something claustrophobic about a life lived entirely in a tower block. It brought back bad memories. Philip was striding in the direction of the crime scene and she almost ran after him.

He looked back at her. 'Why don't you see Mrs Bello to get the list, and we meet at the social worker's office?' She nodded and watched as he continued to frown at the hilly mounds, looming up like tiny graves.

Five

Toks was in the lobby of Mrs Bello's building, waiting for the lift, when the entrance door opened and a young man stepped in. He looked about 22, with a pointed elfin face, long-limbed body and shaggy brown hair. He reminded her of a hyena and smelt like one too. His presence began to needle her. He eyed her with icy pale eyes that made her shiver inwardly. She pretended not to notice. The lift opened with a 'ping' and she entered. He followed. She hesitated before pressing the button for Mrs Bello's floor. Someone had thoughtfully covered it in dripping phlegm. She stepped back and he pressed floor 13. He still maintained his scrutiny in the lift and this time she decided to stare back. The arctic look had become full blast and she refused to flinch. He finally looked away. She sighed under her breath as he stepped off. The door started to close behind him when she heard his whispered snarl. '*Dirty bitch.*'

She dismissed it. It was not a time for confrontation. She knocked on Mrs Bello's door.

'Who is it?' asked a querulous voice.

'Detective Ade,' she answered.

Toks heard the bolts opening and Mrs Bello let her in. Her face looked drawn and unhappy.

'Good afternoon, Ma,' she greeted.

'Good afternoon,' the woman answered as she led Toks to the sitting room.

'Please sit down.'

Toks did.

'I'm very worried about my granddaughter. Everyone is talking about that child's hand you found. Whose is it? Is there someone kidnapping Black children and killing them? Has this person taken Venus?'

Her reddened eyes filled with tears. 'It is only me and those children. Only me and them!'

'We're trying everything possible, Ma, but we need your help. I need you to tell me more about Venus, and I need the list we talked about.'

Mrs Bello's face turned bitter. 'What else do you want to know? I've told you everything. You just need to look for her.'

Toks ignored her outburst.

'Did she ever complain about anything or anyone she played with, at home or school?'

'Why would she complain? She is a strong, stubborn child who likes to play with all these estate children.' She looked thoughtful. 'There was a boy that she said was always troubling her.'

'Which boy?'

'He comes to play with all of them downstairs and wanted Venus to go to his house but she refused. He hit her.'

42

'What did you do?'

'I was very angry. He scratched her face. She had red marks all over. Venus is *very* light-skinned.'

'This boy. Do you know his name?'

'No. Even Venus didn't know his name. She says he comes to play all the time. I told her to stay away from those people. This estate is not good for them but they will not re-house us.' Her voice was filled with self-pity.

'Is Joseph at home? I would like to speak to him again.'

'No, he's at school. He is well now.'

Toks stood up.

'I need the list, Ma.'

'What for?'

'By speaking to everyone she knows we can remove them from our list.'

'I have phoned everyone. Venus is not there and she would not go anywhere without my permission.'

'We still need your help to speak to these people. It will help our investigation.'

'Ok,' she conceded, and with a grunt heaved herself from the chair. 'Officer. You're very respectful and I like that,' she said. 'Our children come to this country and become lost. Please try to help me, o. She is too young to be lost like this. She has no mother or father to look out for her except me. Wait here, I will prepare the list.'

She left Toks in the sitting room and came back with a piece of paper and a pen. Toks watched as she sat heavily on a chair and slowly began to write. Toks took out her notepad and began to make some quick notes.

'Here,' said Mrs Bello. Toks put away her notepad.

'This is 3 names, my son and my daughter and a cousin. But Venus will not have seen any of them. We most of the time talk only on the phone.'

Toks did not want to dwell on things that could have happened to the girl. Unless Venus ran away, the alternative would be devastating news for her grandmother.

'Thank you, ma,' she said as she took the piece of paper. Mrs Bello walked her to the door and stepped into the hallway with her. When the lift came, she waved her off and then carefully locked her door.

Toks checked the time and noted that she had only 10 minutes to spare before the appointment with the social worker. She saw Philip tapping his foot outside of the office.

'Any luck?' His eyes probed hers.

'Yes, thank goodness. She also mentioned a mysterious boy that comes to play with the children and at one point had scratched Venus on the face. It might be worth asking the children about him.'

The social services building was a massive two-story block with a lobby that smelt of damp. The receptionist, a sulky girl with smooth brown skin and hair in tiny twists, told them that the social worker was running late. She directed them to a set of aged chairs.

Toks looked around with interest. The carpet was a gloomy grey, the walls a strange green colour – a cross between slime or vomit. As they sat down, the main door opened and a slender woman entered. She had thick black hair cut in an expensive bob. She glanced at the receptionist, managing to wave to her despite being weighed down by a hefty briefcase and files, and walked over to them.

'Hello, I'm Mary Grant. Sorry I'm late.'

'I'm Detective Dean and this is Detective Ade.' He automatically extended his hand for a handshake.

'Sorry,' she grimaced at her load. 'Please follow me.'

She led them to a small cubicle with plastic chairs.

'Please sit down. I'll be back in a minute. I need to get the children's file.' She left and came back with a bulging folder.

'Right. It's all very worrying. Especially with what's happening around there at the moment.'

'We're doing everything to find her,' said Philip. 'Her description has been sent everywhere, but we need more background details. Mother, father....'

'Venus and Joseph are twins, as you know. No known father. They lived with their mother until the age of 4, when they were placed in care. Their mother had developed severe mental illness from chronic drug abuse and was sectioned, but not before the children had been physically and sexually abused. It was hard to pin down which of their mother's boyfriends was the culprit, but we eventually did and he is now in jail. Their grandmother came forward and offered to look after them, and here we are today.' Toks took rapid notes as Mary Grant spoke.

'Recently, we decided to separate them.' That got Tok's attention. 'According to the grandmother, she caught them 'together'. They were under the covers in a very compromising manner. Children experiment, especially those with their kind of history, and it would have been sufficient to put some therapy in place for them, but Mrs Bello asked me to remove Venus from her home. She blamed her for 'entrapping' Joseph. She wanted us to place her somewhere else as soon as possible. I found a placement for Venus but now that she has disappeared, that's likely to fall through. To be honest with you, we suspect she might have run away.'

'How did she feel about leaving her grandmother and friends?' asked Toks.

'Not too happy. We explained that she would see her grandmother and brother on planned visits.'

'We are going to visit their mother. Is there no more information about the father?' asked Philip.

'Venus's grandmother claims her daughter had the children with some Lebanese or Arab businessman who frequently travelled to the UK. She said that as soon as her daughter told him about the pregnancy he disappeared. She already suffered from bipolar so I think this tipped her over.'

She glanced at her watch—a broad masculine one with a dark brown strap—and said, 'I'm sorry but I have another appointment.' They stood up. 'Please let me know as soon as you hear anything.'

'Definitely,' answered Philip.

***

Coretta sat in her minimalist study and eyed her MacBook screen. The small room consisted of a shaggy, deep pile rug, a glass computer desk, and the chair. She tried to be paperless but despaired of the endless letters that still came through the post. She had a virtual assistant but still preferred to do her own paperwork. She wondered if she should employ admin help once or twice a week but dismissed that. Besides, she was only at the beginning of this new investigation. She sighed and mentally prepared herself for the ordeal of her parents-in-law's anniversary dinner. She was already dressed. The door opened and Richard came in.

'Coretta, we need to get a move on. We're expected for eight,' he said.

He came behind her chair and roped his arms around her. 'Are you okay? You look pale.'

She smiled. 'Why shouldn't I be? I'm about to *suffer* your mum for the evening.'

Richard chuckled. Coretta stood up and gripped his waist. She was 5'5 to his 6'2. He was tall and lean with curly brown hair.

She stroked his face. 'I do love you. You know that.'

'I love you too.' He held her close and tipped her head back. 'We could give the other thing a chance?'

She avoided his eyes and tried to move away. She knew he was referring to adopting a child after ten years together and no pregnancy. 'I know, Richard. I just wanted to see a little me and you, a child that is ours. I know it's selfish.'

'Look at me.' She did. Her eyes met his imploring ones. 'I

know this isn't really the time for this, but we need to give it more serious thought. Maybe slow down a bit? We don't really need the money.'

She pulled away. 'If we don't go now your mum will definitely blame me for our lateness.'

'I want you to think about it. Let's take a different step.' He pulled her back. 'A different journey.'

Coretta pressed her lips together. 'We'll discuss it later. Promise.' She stood on tiptoe and pulled his head down to hers.

Six

After a quick progress meeting with the team, Philip and Toks went to visit Fatia, Venus's mum, at her residential home.

She lived on Bostall Street, SW1—a long street with rows of pricey houses. Toks eyed the rows of expensive cars and wondered how the residents felt about their 'special' neighbours in No 91.

Philip sighed as he circled the road for the second time before sliding into a space vacated by a sleek BMW. He ignored the sign that said parking was permitted for residents only. They walked to the house and ascended the concrete steps that led to a dark green door with a bold, metal '91' screwed on. The doorbell rang a melodious song and a woman with a pale freckled face and purple hair opened the door and gave them a shy smile.

'Hello, I'm Detective Dean.' He showed his warrant card. 'This is Detective Ade. We called and spoke to Edwin Macletton about visiting Fatia Bello this afternoon.'

She nodded vigorously. 'Yes, Edwin told me. My name is Daisy.' She spoke in a soft, halting voice. 'Please come in.

Fatia's expecting you.'

She led them through a square hallway to a shabby front room furnished with leather brown chairs and a bookshelf. A lady with straggly, dark hair sat close to a large TV and watched the music channel with a hang-jawed, blank expression. She ignored them and started to sway to the loud music.

'Please, sit down,' said Daisy. 'I'll be back in a minute.' She left the room and Philip followed her, whispering something before coming back in. Madam 'Straggly Hair' gave a big yawn and then let out a loud fart. Toks held her breath before exhaling loudly. The ripe, rotten smell hung all around them.

'She's going to find us a quiet room,' said Philip.

'Good idea,' she said, as more squelchy farts escaped the resident. At this rate she might poo on herself, thought Toks. Philip's lip lifted in a slight smile as he caught the look on her face.

Daisy came back. 'She's waiting for you in the dining area. It's quiet at this time of the day.' They followed her to a large room with wooden flooring and a long dining table. Sat at one end was a large woman with bushy, knotted afro hair and ashy, dry skin. A good Vaseline would solve that problem, Toks thought. Fatia was nodding her head as she looked at them with dull eyes.

'Hello, Fatia. I'm Detective Dean and this is Detective Ade. We've come to have a little chat with you.'

Silence.

'Hello,' said Toks.

The silence continued and it was almost a shock when she

finally spoke in a deep, husky whisper.

'Have you got any cigarettes, Sugar?' She looked Toks up slowly, her eyes stripping off layers of her clothing, leaving her naked.

Toks maintained her straight face.

'You look luscious. Good enough to eat. Breasts made to suckle.' She turned to Philip. 'You! Don't you think Sugar good enough to eat? Would you like to eat her? I would!'

Toks sat still.

'We don't have cigarettes,' he said. 'And I suggest you don't talk to Detective Ade like that. We have a few questions for you.'

A crafty look replaced the dull one. *'Then,* I won't talk to *you.* I prefer to talk to Sugar. Want to go to another room, Sugar?'

Toks leaned very close to her and as her nose filled with nicotine and the acrid sweat of the woman's unwashed body, she said, 'Look, Fatia, enough of that. We came to talk to you. You will get a cigarette if you tell us what we want. Alright?'

She seemed to contemplate what Toks said then started to tear at a dirty long nail with her row of discoloured teeth.

'Ok. Cigarettes after you talk to me, Sugar. Is it about Venus?'

Toks couldn't hide her start. Philip waited. 'She's in trouble, isn't she? Always knew she would get in trouble. Too forward. Dirty little girl! Very naughty. How about my thief of a mother? Call herself a good Muslim woman, eh? Three of us by three different fathers.' She gave Toks a broad wink. 'That's my mama. Venerable Mrs Bello.'

'Yes, it's about Venus,' said Philip. 'Has anyone asked about her then?'

Fatia checked the torn nail. 'No.'

'When did you last see her?'

She eyed them and snarled, 'My thief of a mother never brings them. I have not seen them in a long time. She said they are *trauma*tised.'

'How can we reach their father?' asked Toks.

Her eyes seemed to flame up. 'The bastard that left me alone to feed two children? I hope he rots in hell. He ran away back to his wife in Nigeria, or Ghana or wherever! I don't care. I don't want to ever see him again! Can I have my cigarette now?'

'You've not answered my question.'

'I want my cigarette. You promised!' Her eyes glinted. 'Give me my cigarette. Throw in Sugar over there and I'll sing some more for you.'

Philip brought out a stick but did not give it to her. 'I have the cigarette. What can you tell us?'

She heaved off the chair and leaned over the table, her heavy breasts straining through her stained shift dress. Toks could see the sparse dark hair that sprouted from her chin. 'Give me that cigarette,' she roared. 'It's mine! Stop asking about that dirty girl. Give me!'

A man and woman rushed into the room. The man with close cropped hair looked at them. 'Daisy is waiting for you in the office. First turning on the left.' He turned to Fatia. 'Come on, let's go and sit in the garden.' She beamed at him.

***

The office was a cramped little space with a large desk strewn with papers, a filing cabinet and hardly any room for chairs. Daisy, who was scribbling on a notepad, stood up as they entered.

'I hope it was useful talking to her.'

'Not really,' said Philip. 'We didn't get much out of her. Could you tell me if she's had any visitors in the last three weeks?'

She shook her head.

'Only her mother. Once every two months. She does get phone calls. Her mum calls her once a week. Sometimes her brother.'

'What's his name? Do you have an address for him? Also, do you know when he last called?'

She went to a cabinet, opened a folder, and copied out some information on a piece of paper. She looked thoughtful as she handed it to Philip.

'Fatia docs tend to talk a lot about her daughter. Especially in her lucid moments.'

'What impression does she give you about her?' asked Philip.

She leaned towards them and whispered. 'I think she hates that poor little girl.'

'Thank you for your time,' he said, solemnly.

At the front door a slim, young girl with wild unfocused eyes blocked their way.

'Fuck me, Daisy. Who're this? Fuck it. You know all visitors have to stay and watch a film with us.'

'Cathy, language, please! Go to the lounge and I'll be there in a minute.' Daisy's voice was calm and authoritative. The girl reluctantly moved to the side.

She opened the door and let them out.

Seven

Coretta suppressed her excitement as she drove to her appointment in Peckham. She had been close-mouthed about it to Richard. If she had told him she was going anywhere near South East London he would have asked to come with her. That man imagined that shootings took place at every corner of the street! She really needed a breakthrough and this contact might yield something. Google maps told her she had reached her destination. It was a pity that it had taken her through unnecessary twists and turns first. The man she had arranged to meet was a contact of a contact. He had sounded pretty cagey on the phone. She came out of the car and clutched her voluminous woolly coat to her body. It was only about seven, yet the night was decidedly chilly. She resisted the urge to check that her handbag had the small recorder that doubled as a video camera when she needed it. She preferred to use this to a phone. They had agreed to meet at a restaurant. He had said he would be wearing jeans, a shirt and a cap. Him and one thousand other men, she thought. They would find each other somehow. She entered the restaurant, happy to leave the outside chill for the cosy space which smelt deliciously of Nigerian food. It had a small bar area manned by a young man in a waiter's white and black. She realised it had been a while since she'd eaten. They had agreed that the bar would be their meeting point. She saw a man in jeans and shirt watching her and hoped this was him.

'Saul?' she asked softly. He inclined his head and stood up. He was thickset. Looked about 32.

'Madam Williams?' Coretta nodded. She never used her real name in these meetings. 'Let us walk to the back,' he said. 'I have reserved seats for us.' She was glad that she wore trainers, otherwise her heels would have been clattering on the smooth wooden floor. The place seemed to be attracting good custom. He led her to the back of the room. Once they sat down he quickly looked around. 'You can never be too careful these days,' he said.

He assessed her and she eyed him back. She had learnt from long ago that a bold stare does the job of getting people to take her seriously. His openly challenging and admiring looks turned serious and he dropped his eyes.

'You told me that you know what happened to the boy who was found in the Thames and will give me a name.' She got directly to the point.

'Yes, I do.' His voice grew brisk and business-like. 'Before we continue, my fee for providing you with this information is 2K. Once you agree, we can talk.'

Coretta did not blink. '£200 is all I can pay you for what you are about to tell me. And I have to even think it's worth that as well.'

He might be working in a wealthy household or know someone who does. She had met many like him before and knew how to deal with them. His information was the beginning of her investigation and she was not about to blow a couple of thousand on something that might not lead her to the end of her search.

He inclined his head again and grinned, exposing uneven teeth. She could see a glimmer of new respect showing in his eyes. 'Fine. The British police blundered their investigation of that murdered boy, that is why they could never find his real killers. They got as far as tracking down a possible village where he came from and then found nothing. As usual, they always think they *know* it all. People trafficking is a billion-pound business and cannot just disappear overnight.' He stopped abruptly. 'I have a name for you.' Coretta brought out her notebook and pen.

'Victor Essam. He knows someone who was smuggled in by a big ring and survived. I cannot take you straight to the person, but call him. He will take you.' He recited a mobile number. She had her recorder as a backup anyway, aware of the partly opened bag between them.

'If you want to learn about people who organise the smugglers, you have got to go to Nigeria. It is a big business with some powerful people involved. They will kill you instantly and nobody will find your body. The boy they found was an exception. There are thousands who just disappear. Life is precious. Blood is the biggest commodity in the world. Greater than diamond, oil. You sell a child or a person and the people can do whatever they want. Keep them as a slave to some paedophile, kill them…anything. That is power! The people who killed him had to do it that way to make the *juju* more powerful. And they were confident that the police would not catch them. And have they? These are members of powerful cults who have signed a binding pact.' He eyed her. 'You *do* know what I mean? Have you read Revelation in the bible?'

She shook her head. His tone became patronising. 'It's not just a matter of money, but of the soul. These people are preparing for the days the evil beast will rule the earth. They want to be part of the ruling power when it happens. Now I hear that the police found that poor child's hand in Hackney. People say it is like the boy. They never found his limbs or even the head.' He shrugged. 'Who knows? Just speak to Victor.'

'Call him,' commanded Coretta. She gave him her phone. 'Tell him about me.'

He gave her a long, considering stare. 'Madam Williams. You don't trust me? The man that recommended me is your trusted contact.'

'I just need you to let him know that I'm here.' Coretta's voice was firm.

He reluctantly took the phone from her. 'Hey, Victor? I have that madam with me. She wants to talk to you.'

He gave her back the phone.

'Hello?' The voice on the other end of the phone was low and soft. 'Madam? Good evening. I will text you the address that you will need to come to. Please bring money. Bye, bye, madam.' The line went dead.

Coretta turned back to her contact.

He leaned closer. 'Be very careful. Are you a Christian, or even religious?'

'Why?' she challenged. She rummaged through her bag for the cash.

'Because the path you're following, you need to be a very strong Christian, Muslim or strong non-believer. You know some people say they don't believe in anything. And truly they don't.'

She handed him his money.

'Good luck, madam. Be very careful.' He stood up and was quickly out of the restaurant. She stared at the empty space he had just vacated.

Eight

With no real progress on their investigations, Toks was able to attend church. Praise and worship was where she experienced the most peace. Soon, the Sunday morning service was over. The pastor and his wife, originally from Zimbabwe, were intelligent and charismatic people. This church, a big domed building with cushioned pews that could easily accommodate a few hundred people, was a vast improvement from where they had previously worshiped. The congregation had contributed a great deal of money to build this one and it was worth it.

'How are you doing, Sis Toks?' She stood up as Pastor John approached her. He gave her a quick hug. 'We missed seeing you last week.' He was taller than Toks and rather good looking.

'I missed coming here as well. It's just been busy, sir.'

'How is the new posting? Are you settling in well?'

'Too well!' She answered, countering her words with a grimace. She knew she could not keep him talking for too long as a lot of people were waiting. He clasped her hand briefly. 'Just know you're always in our prayers.'

'Thank you.'

His attention was diverted by another church member and Toks went to his wife, an elegant slight woman who always made her feel like an Amazonian. Today she was wearing an especially colourful, long traditional skirt and embroidered top sent by her mum and felt even bigger.

'I like your outfit. It shows off your lovely curves,' the pastor's wife said, her light brown eyes sparkling with mischief. 'I must try and get a few myself. But I want you to teach me how to cook that *jollof rice* and *moin moin*. Pastor loves it. Getting one to one lesson from you will be better than YouTube. They just never turn out well!'

'We'll make a date,' Toks promised.

The other woman's eyes softened. 'I know you're very busy but I'd like to see you more often at the women's meetings.'

'The times seem to always clash with when I am on duty,' said Toks.

'Just try when you can, please.'

'I will,' she promised.

Bode joined them and they said their goodbyes.

'That was really good playing,' she told him. He had skilfully and discreetly accompanied the solo singers in the service. His keyboard skills were improving and Toks was glad that she had insisted on all those lessons long ago. She had felt really proud of him. He shrugged but she knew he was pleased.

'I've been doing some practice recently.'

'I know.' She looked around. The church was emptying.

'I thought Darren was here today,' she said. His friend Darren had been attending the service with them for a couple of months now.

'He's busy today.'

'Shall we go to Chang Palace or Maharashi or do Nigerian?'

'Chang, Mum.' He grinned. 'You know I like my Chinese anytime over Indian or Nigerian. It's nice to be spoilt for choice.'

'Chang it is then.'

Much later, after a huge meal of Chow mein, beef and black bean sauce, huge king prawns in sweet and sour sauce followed by a large glass of coke, Toks sat back and grinned at Bode and he grinned back. The guilt would come later.

'Look at you,' she said. 'Thin as a rake, and look at me! You're a bad influence!'

'Oh Mum,' he rolled his eyes. 'You're fine.'

'Have you seen my spare tyres?' She eyed her belly. She giggled and they started laughing. She loved their Sunday afternoon rituals. It was boring going back to food at home after church, so they went for their Sunday lunches wherever they chose.

Toks stopped when she saw Bode's face go serious. 'Mum?'

'Yes, son.' She became attentive.

'I think I'd like to meet my dad now.'

She went still. This was new. She looked at a face that was a younger version of his dad's and realised this moment was inevitable. Fear lanced through her. He could meet Femi and love him more than her. It almost brought tears to her eyes.

But looking at him, she also saw the son she had raised. She sighed. He was right. As much as she hated Femi, she could not deprive Bode of his father.

'Are you sure?' She searched for his hand under the table and was surprised when he gripped hers. It was serious. She gave another sigh. 'I will arrange it.'

'Thanks, Mum.'

***

Philip picked a paper from those scattered on his desk and peered at it. He had googled rituals around the world, especially West Africa, and coupled with the papers from the Alpha torso files from 2001 it made for gory reading. Was Venus's disappearance connected to this? The girl was friendly with the local boys on the estate and it was a higher possibility that she ran away. Philip hoped nothing more sinister had taken place. He closed his eyes. He had two cases on his hand. It would be great if they could find Venus and solve that one quickly. They had enough staff working day and night to find the girl. Katherine Gardner and Pete Boxley from child protection were good detectives, but Katherine was another headache to deal with. Even when he had been married to Helen all those years ago, Katherine's logic and her cold fire had still attracted him. Philip snuffed the thoughts. He recalled his last visit to the morgue to see Dr Rothman. He had watched her surrounded by empty trolleys as she stared at a series of x-ray charts and photographs on a wall. She had given him an unsmiling look and then started speaking.

'This is similar to Alpha, but not the same. The cut to her hand is different from that made on him.' She exhaled and looked at him. 'This child had been abused.' She pointed, 'Look carefully.' Philip peered at each x-ray showing the hand in different positions. 'Her fingers had been broken in different places. Some of those breaks are old and some fresh.'

She moved away from the x-rays to a trolley. Philip gazed at the tiny decomposed hand. It was hard to equate it with anything at the moment. The skin was very dark. She turned it palm up. 'See that? There are burn marks all over it like someone had pressed it on a hot hob.' The palm did look scoured. The tremor in Rothman's voice surprised him. She was not liberal with her emotions. 'We're waiting to get more results so I should be able to tell you more in a couple of days.' He stared at the back she firmly turned to him.

'Thanks, Olive,' he said softly and left.

As he sat now, gazing at the papers strewn on his desk, it felt like he was clutching at straws. He lifted a small glass of cognac to his lips. It was four in the morning. He would be visiting Emily later on. Calls from the home said she had given them a rough week. The thought of facing her when she was in that manic state twisted his guts.

Nine

At work on Monday, Toks brooded at the thought of working with Katherine and 'Roly Poly' Pete. They were two over-swollen egos that she could do without. She watched Philip loping his way to her desk and immediately repaired the scowl on her face. His face was unshaven as usual and he had dark shadows jostling for position with the bags under his eyes.

He stood and watched her and it dawned on her that he had somehow gleaned her worry about Katherine and Roly Poly.

'Katherine and Pete are very experienced officers and there's a lot you can learn from them. I'll get you to do some shadowing with Katherine.'

'Thanks.' She tried to smile.

'I'd like us to chat about how you've done so far, maybe go to Chris's Café after this interview? Are you partial to all day breakfast, egg, bacon?'

Toks grimaced and invisibly patted the rolls of fat under her skirt suit. It was her love of all-day breakfast that got her this big. 'I love all day breakfast,' she almost whispered in guilt.

He gave a small smile. 'So do I. Now, about Brian Cody. He's a nasty, clever bastard, so be careful with him. He's agreed to come in for questioning. I'm not surprised. He loves to get under our skin. He's been in and out of trouble his whole life and knows his way around the law. It doesn't help that he comes from a very wealthy family.' He laughed bitterly. 'Whoever tells you that money means nothing, lies. All they need to do is buy the best lawyers. Are you still ok to lead?'

She nodded.

Brian Cody was waiting for them, slouched in a chair, drumming his long thin fingers on the table. She looked around the room with its single table, chairs, and recorders, to ensure all was ready. She ignored the irritating tapping sounds he was making and sat opposite him. Philip moved his chair closer. Brian Cody, with his smooth baby face, dark pony tail and preppy outfit, was a 35-year-old convicted paedophile with a lengthy file. He had recently finished a 5-year sentence. She turned on the recorders, then said their names, date, time and asked him to identify himself.

'Brian Cody,' he said, his voice light and amused.

She kept her cool, aware that DCI Jackson and DSupt Amos were having a meeting and waiting for them to report back.

'So, you've finally condescended to come and question me? I've told you that I've done nothing.'

'Witnesses have seen you chatting to children near Cedar estate,' she said.

He gave her a long, considering look and then nodded to

himself as if taking in information.

'Sweetheart, I know you've got to do their work for them, but concentrate your effort somewhere else. You're a Black woman. They don't like you.'

Toks ignored him.

'Cody,' said Philip. 'Is there something you need to tell us?'

'Look, it's a free world and I can go wherever I want to within reason. I have neither been near the estate nor chatted to any of the children. I'm not allowed to.'

'You just came back from Thailand,' said Philip.

She saw Cody's slight twitch of surprise, but he recovered very quickly. 'So, what!'

'Your trust fund can only take you so far, Cody. We know Mum and Dad would do anything for you. Including setting you up in Thailand.' Philip continued to stare at Cody, his expression blank. Toks admired that.

'It's not anybody's business where I go. I've served my time. Okay?'

Toks noticed that he was beginning to lose the carefully constructed cool.

'A little girl has recently gone missing. Would you know anything about it?'

'I don't *do* little girls.' Toks felt goose pimples rise on her arms. She wanted to yell and smash the smugness from his face. His voice had grown languorous again as he eyed them insolently.

'You have been seen around that estate. A little girl is

missing. Answer us, now!' she shouted.

'If you want answers so much, why come to me? Is it not the same area that you found a child's severed hand? Obviously, whoever did that could have taken this girl. You people are looking in the wrong place.'

He turned to Toks. 'Sweetheart, I lived in Ghana, Cameroon and Haiti a long time ago. You're African, aren't you? You should know better.' He shrugged his shoulders and winked at her. 'Maybe this is *juju*. I can't give you what you require. If someone has chopped up another Black child, it's definitely not me. Besides, if you've read my file, then you should know that this is not me. Go back and search who you need to search. I'm not your killer.'

'Who told you we're looking for a killer?' asked Philip, quick as a rattlesnake. 'We're not finished with you, Cody. You know how *enjoyable* prison is. There are people waiting there who hate child abusers like you. I'm sure they'll pass you hand to hand and tear your arse open till you beg for mercy, then discard you. Understand me?' Brian Cody looked rattled then quickly recovered.

'That is no news to me. I have paid my dues.'

'Now, Cody,' continued Philip. 'If you have anything to tell us, let us know now.'

'You've turned my house upside down. You've searched all you can. You know I have nothing to do with this. Why don't you start concentrating on the Africans and their *jujus* and leave me alone? You can see that I chose to speak to you without my lawyer present. That is a measure of my goodwill.

Now, please let me go.'

Toks looked at the video camera. 'Interview terminated.'

Philip gestured to her and they stepped outside the room. DCI Jackson and DSupt Amos joined them. Philip quickly filled them in.

'Release him,' Amos said. 'We have no proof. Besides, his M.O. are young, white boys.'

'You're right, guv. Well done, both of you,' said DCI Jackson. 'We'll do it two ways.' He pointed to the closed interview room. 'Philip, kick him out for now. He'll be back inside in no time, trust fund or not. Let's comb through that list from the grandma with a toothpick. I want us to go back to those local families. If there is a connection between the two cases, it will come soon. Trust me, something will jump out and smack us.'

Ten

Coretta played with Richard's curly head of hair as it laid pressed against her chest.

'Richard?'

'Hmm?'

'That was great.'

'You want some more?' he smiled.

She chuckled. 'I'm aching all over!'

'So?'

'Remember how your mum ignored me when we finally showed up?'

'She was giving you the 'Ice Queen' treatment. You should feel worthy.'

They both laughed. 'On a more serious note.' Coretta sat up and pulled the quilt to cover her chest.

Richard groaned. 'Don't spoil our fun.'

'Richard!'

'Ok. Talk.'

'How far have you gone with your *juju* research?' Richard leaned against the pillow and covered himself. Coretta knew she had his full attention now.

'Not very far. Why?'

'I need some information on ritual killing. Have you come across material on that?'

'Yes.' His voice was guarded.

'I just need a general idea. Remember that boy they found in the Thames years ago? It was ritual killing.'

'I have some research on him.' He leaned forward and pulled her face close. 'Please tell me that you're not doing anything dangerous. You know the police never found the boy's killers. They're still around somewhere.'

'Look, I'm not after killers. I just need background material, that's all. Instead of me trawling the internet, I know you'll probably have first rate info.'

She was feeling a bit impatient with his over-protectiveness, but refused to let it show.

Richard folded his arms across the bed cover and she knew their moment of romance had taken a backseat. For now.

'Ok. Here it is. Ritual killing never went away and seems to be on the rise.' His voice was low and scratchy. 'It's big in Africa, Haiti and parts of South America. Some twisted people are even trying to use the blood of children as witch-craft medicine to cure AIDs! It's called Muti in South Africa. Hundreds of children go missing. It's almost daily in countries like Zambia, Nigeria, Cameroon – to name a few. Bodies are discovered with parts missing. The most potent, for whatever gain they require, are penises, breasts, tongues, brains, eyes... Corrupt politicians and the wealthy have joined cults, and the highest demand is human sacrifice. There are also the body parts markets… parts smuggled to Asia or within Africa and sold to the highest wealthy bidder.'

Coretta watched his faraway look. *What was she getting herself into?*

He continued. 'A man was recently discovered in Nigeria with human heads in the trunk of his car. Quite a lot of people would have been involved. It's big business.' He pulled her head to his chest. 'It's bad. Here we have serial killers. In Africa they have their serial killers too, but they have practical reasons for the killings.' He took her hand and absently traced a pattern on her palm. 'You asked for it. I've got a lot of stuff in the study, but it makes gory reading. Your human traffickers are sometimes just conduits for people who have more terrible intentions.'

Coretta was quiet for a long time as she pulled him close. 'Do you have to do this?' she asked.

'I'm researching *juju* for my presentation, aren't I? I can't do that without touching ritual killing.' He turned her face up and looked in her eyes. 'My question is why are you asking all these questions, Coretta? What are you up to this time?'

***

Toks wondered about Venus as she made her journey to Surrey. Philip had agreed that Toks could follow up with Venus's uncle as he was the contact for Mrs Bello. She hadn't made an appointment; she liked the element of surprise. Her mind went back to Venus. It's like the girl had just vanished. No sightings, no witnesses, no CCTV footage. The uniforms had combed the estate, but nothing. Surely if the girl had run away they would have found something. Could she have been abducted? Her phone had been left at home and the last person she had called had been her friend, Teresa.

Toks arrived in Surrey within an hour and drove through the private road that led to Mr Bello's home. A huge building eased into view behind majestic trees and well-shorn shrubs. She imagined that the white gravel loudly crunching under her tyres would surely announce the arrival of her modest car. Its noise reminded her of her childhood home in Nigeria where it signalled her parent's arrival from work or travel and a scramble to hide any mischief. She jerked herself back to the present and tried to recall the house's name written on the wooden plaque by the road she just came through. Yes, 'The Biscay'. No number. She parked her car beside a black Mercedes and a metallic silver Porsche. The rain had stopped and the air was fresh. She didn't recall her neighbourhood in Dagenham smelling like this. Maybe if she won the lottery she could move to this area of Surrey. Mr Shola Bello's music career must be highly successful. She walked to the solid oak front door etched with intricate African carvings and rang the bell. It probably cost her whole year's salary. Why were his mother, nephew and niece living in a crime-ridden council estate if he was so well-off?

A tiny, young Filipino woman with short dark hair opened the door. 'Yes? Can I help?' Her voice was cool and wary, her accent heavy.

'I'm Detective Ade.' Toks showed her warrant card. 'I'd like to see Mr Bello, please.'

The maid did not look at the warrant. 'He not here. Who are you?'

'Police.'

The maid's eyes widened as she looked Toks up and down. 'Wait. I speak to Mrs Bello. Wait.' She shut the door. When it opened again a tall, thin woman came out. She had straight blonde hair and lovely delicate features marred only by her too-thin lips.

'Mrs Bello?'

'Yes. My maid said you're the police?'

'Yes, ma'am. I would like to see your husband, please.'

She arched her eyebrow. 'Can I see your ID?'

Toks showed her card which Mrs Bello spent a few minutes examining.

'Come in,' she said at last, and led her through a hallway with a tall arched ceiling and into a sitting room with polished wood flooring, egg-yellow settees, and some yellow-hued paintings on the wall.

'Sit down, please,' she said, and gracefully sank into one of the chairs. Toks envied her poise. She guessed it took a lot of money to obtain such confidence. 'I'm Casey Bello. Shola is away. What's this about?'

'It's about his niece. You do know she's missing?'

'Yes, we do. But how can we help?'

'We understand she and her brother Joseph stay with you

sometimes.'

She arched her eyebrow again. It seemed to be a habit. 'They haven't stayed with us in a few years.'

'May I ask why?'

'You will have to ask my husband that question.'

'How would you describe Venus and her brother?'

'They are lovely children and adore their cousin, my son, Jason.'

'Were you never curious as to why they stopped coming?'

'I respected my husband's wishes.'

'When will he be back?'

'In two weeks.'

'Could you confirm whether he was in the country at the time Venus went missing?'

'No. Shola has been away for three months. I can assure you he has not been in touch with his mother since that time. I'm surprised you even have our address. Who gave it to you?'

'Your mother-in-law. We're talking to all of Venus's relatives and you're her nearest.'

'Sorry, we cannot be of much help. I do hope you find Venus quickly.' She stood up. 'Shola is quite upset about it.'

Yeah, right!

'Can you describe your relationship with your mother-in-law?'

Her thin lips curled. 'It's fine. You've met my mother-in-law. She is what she is.'

'And that is?'

'She loves her son. I love my husband.'

'Is that a problem?'

She smiled but it did not reach her eyes. 'It is a question you will need to ask her.'

'Are there any questions you are able to answer now?'

'I have nothing more to say, detective.'

A little boy of about four ran into the room. He had brown curls and a face that reminded Toks of Venus's twin brother, Joseph.

'Hello, sweetie.' His mother bent down to give him a cuddle. I thought you were colouring with Martha.'

The maid came in. 'Jason. Come with me. Let's finish. Mummy busy.' She glanced at them nervously.

Jason ignored her as he tugged at his mum's skirt. 'Don't worry, Martha,' Casey Bello said as she scooped him up and led the way back to the front door. She turned to Toks. 'Sorry, I couldn't be of more help.'

'When Mr Bello is back in the country, tell him to give me a call, please.'

Toks gave her a card.

***

Philip Dean kept his promise. After briefing him about her visit to the Bellos, he invited Toks to Chris's Café down the road from the station. It's where most of the officers went for their daily dose of cholesterol loaded breakfast. The owner, Chris, originally from Lithuania, ran an efficient business with his wife Justina and their adult children. Justina, in her late fifties, friendly with faded blonde hair and a gentle smile, came to them with her little notepad.

'Hello, Officer Philip. What can I get you today?'

Philip smiled. 'Justina. The usual. Egg on toast with a strong cup of coffee. Toks?'

She had been thinking of going all out for the all-day breakfast. After all, she argued with herself, she had that supermarket salad waiting for her in the fridge back home. She also had the prawn rich Nigerian fried rice she cooked for Bode which she promised herself not to touch.

'All day breakfast,' gulped Toks.

'Sausage or bacon?'

'Bacon, please. Can I have hot water to go with it?' She was happy with that. The hot water would wash away the fat, she hoped.

Justina left and Toks felt Philip's intense scrutiny. 'Are you ok?' he asked.

'Yes, I am.'

'How do you feel about swimming in the deep end of detective work?'

'Fine. I think we're doing well.'

He nodded. 'You're doing very well. It's not anyone's fault, but we have lost time. We're splashed all over the news and haven't come near to finding a missing 9-year-old or the murderers and torturers of a 4-year-old.'

'It's complex.'

'The most complex cases are the simplest. How is your son taking your continued absence?'

She shrugged her shoulders. 'He's used to it.'

He steepled his fingers under his chin. He seemed to be weighing something up.

'Teenagehood is a difficult phase. Do you mind me asking about his dad?'

Toks was surprised but she did somehow mind. Perhaps she wanted to retain a myth. But no, she was just another struggling single parent bringing up a teenage son. Why the pretence? And why did he want to know, another voice queried. 'He's asking to meet up with his dad, who's back in Nigeria. They've never met.'

'Are you happy with this?'

'Not really, but I think it's time.'

He nodded. 'That's wise. I have a twin sister. She's not very well.'

Toks waited. Justina's daughter appeared with his food and her massive plate of eggs, bacon, beans, mushroom, tomato and 2 pieces of toast. She sucked in her stomach and they started to eat.

This was strange territory for her. Ten years in the force and she had had various relationships with her superiors. Mostly formal. She didn't know what to make of this new one.

Eleven

Coretta saw Victor Essam vigorously waving at her as soon as she entered the restaurant where they had arranged to meet. He was a small man in an oversized sweater and blue knitted hat. He had set their meeting to eight pm.

She smiled to herself as she realised that she was becoming a proud customer of restaurants in the South East of London. This one was no match to the previous one in Peckham. It was small and shabby with a tired-looking girl of about 18 who sidled up to them as soon as she sat down and asked if she wanted a drink. Coretta felt like declining but saw that Victor was already drinking a bottle of Nigerian Guinness.

'Orange juice, please.' She turned to him. 'Would you like another one, Mr Essam?'

He gave her a happy smile, revealing small ferret teeth.

'Yes, madam. I don't mind. This drink has plenty of iron. I like it very much."

As the waitress left to fetch their drinks, Coretta got straight to the point. 'Saul must have told you what I needed from you,' she said.

'Yes, madam,' he started to speak in a slow whisper. 'I have very good information for you and I can take you to the woman who this thing happened to. You will of course have to give me something for it.'

'Did Saul tell you that I'm trying to investigate human traffickers?'

She watched as he carefully looked around the small, shabby restaurant before leaning across the table.

'He did. The woman who you are going to see will tell you everything about this people. They are terrible, madam. Some are killers. What can the British government do against them? I will need £2000 to take you to this woman.'

'I don't have £2,000. I have £1000 that I can give you.' Coretta winced, but she had to see this woman.

A frown replaced his smile.

'It is £2000, madam. £1000 to see her, and £1000 for the information I'm about to give.'

Coretta paused to think. 'I will give you £1,500.'

He pursed his lips and then suddenly smiled. 'Agreed, madam. Everybody is happy, eh?'

'Tell me what you know, please.'

They stopped when the girl brought their drinks.

'This woman will tell you what she go through at their hand. As for me, the only thing I can tell you is that they are very bold. They have a powerful Chief in Nigeria who is sponsoring. This is big money you know, madam. People back home give them maybe £2000, even £5000, £10,000, so that they can smuggle them here to work, although everything is

becoming more and more difficult day by day. The more difficult the government here make it for people to work, the more
this people will charge.'

'Do you know who is running the operation from here?'

'There is a man called Osasco. I think he is a big man in
this game. He goes to a white garment church in Deptford.
The biggest area is children, but that one is now the most
dangerous. They're not happy about it because they believe
that someone is spoiling business for them. If someone bring
you a child and you sacrifice that child in Thames river, what
do they expect? Now the police are everywhere. They say
Britain is no longer big business.'

Coretta was making quick notes in shorthand as he spoke.
'What's the address of this church in Deptford?'

He wrote something down and gave it to her. 'Now, let's
go.'

'Victor, excuse me for a moment. I need to go to the
ladies.'

In a not so clean toilet, Coretta quickly texted Richard
Victor's number, where she was and his description. He would
try to call her but she would not answer the phone. At least
this was better than nothing.

She returned, sat down and gave him a steady look.
'Victor, it will be difficult for me to follow you like this. I have
only just met you.'

'You will have to trust me, madam.'

'I gathered. For my own safety I have passed your number,
description and our current location to a trusted friend.'

She watched his eyes widen and then he relaxed. 'It is ok, madam. You can never be too careful.'

She gestured for the bill and paid it. She had not touched her drink and was glad she hadn't after seeing the leaky, dirty toilet. Victor drained his glass and picked up the unopened bottle of Guinness. 'I will drink this one at home. Thank you, madam.' He flashed a ferret smile.

She clutched her bag tightly and glanced at her watch as they walked. It was nearly 9. The frigid air had frozen her fingers by the time they got to her car and she fumbled at inserting the key into the door. This was not the first time her investigations had put her in a tight corner. She could imagine Richard's disapproval if he saw her that moment. She had one of those pepper sprays within reach in her purse just in case. They finally got into the car and he directed her through what seemed like a maze of streets. After about 10 minutes, they entered one lined with blocks of flats. He told her to park her car in front of a four-story brick building made up of about 12 flats. He looked around them furtively as they came out. There was no-one in sight. Coretta hoped she was doing the right thing, but kept her right hand inside her bag and near the pepper spray. They climbed concrete steps up to the 3rd floor and walked to a red door. He searched his pockets, brought out some keys and opened the door. She followed him into a room and watched as he switched on the light. It was small, with low lit light and dirty brown sofas. The carpet was brown and worn in places. Coretta was taken aback when she saw the woman in a corner that watched their movements with blank eyes.

'Madam, this is Blessing. She's my younger sister. Please, sit down.'

Coretta sat down. She could see some family resemblance. The woman was tiny and dark-skinned like Victor. 'Blessing.' His voice was soft as he called her gently. 'This is the madam I said I will bring to ask you a few questions.'

'Welcome, madam,' she greeted in a whispery, frail voice. 'What you want to know?'

'Victor says you might be able to tell me of your experience at the hands of the people that brought you to this country.'

'Yes.' Her small eyes still looked vacant and faraway. She turned to her brother who nodded encouragingly. 'They were bad to me. Very bad. My brother pay them so that I can come from back home and stay with him in Britain. They took plenty of money from us and did not bring me to my brother when we arrived. They took me to a big place, like warehouse, with plenty girls. Then after a few days they take me to one man who was very bad. He and many people did bad things to me. They pregnate me. They take my baby.' Her eyes now seemed lit by a hard-inner glow as she spoke. 'They have my baby.'

Hiding her shock, Coretta let the silence continue. 'How did you find your brother?' she asked, at last.

'I run away. I have his address where he live in my head. I say I don't want to be lost in this country so I put the address in my head. And so after a long, long time I manage to run away from that place. I see plenty of white people on the road and ask how to get to my brother. I tell them the address and plenty walk away from me like I was ghost. But one white woman said I was not very far away from my brother and she will help me. God answer my prayer. She tell me how to reach here and give me money. I wait outside this door for my brother to come. He come in the night. I was cold. But he come.' She stopped.

'Do you remember this warehouse they took you to?'

'I listen very good when this bad men talk. When they drink their brandy and smoke their cigarettes and have many girls like me, they talk. They always talk about ackney, ackney. The place they put me with the other girls has rooms, beds, kitchens. But is like warehouse. They always talk and say England is not good business anymore. They say too many laws.' Her eyes pleaded with Coretta. 'Madam, you must find my fine baby. He's a beautiful boy. Find him for me.'

Hackney! 'Do you remember the address of the house?' Coretta did not want any excitement to show in her voice. She might have a breakthrough if she treaded carefully.

'I don't know. Fisburi Park, I hear him tell somebody. I think it is. They never allow me to go out, so I listen very carefully. But they have my baby.'

'Do you know who delivered your baby?'

'A woman come. They say she is nurse. She deliver the baby and take it away.' Her eyes welled up with tears. 'Please, madam. You have to help me find my baby.' She held her hand to her face and started to shake. Coretta tried to hold her hand but she jumped up. She clapped her hands to her head as fat tears gushed down her cheeks. Her brother went to her and whispered in a soothing voice. This seemed to calm her down. He glanced at Coretta, shook his head and then led her out of the room.

'They have nonsensed my sister!' he said when he came back. 'I know the brother of the person that did this to my sister in Nigeria. I cannot write home to our family and tell them this has happened. They will blame me. That man Osasco link with his brother in Nigeria. The brother in Nigeria is called Emmanuel. They said they can help me bring my sister to come and work, but see what they have done to her. They have finished her!'

'Do you know the address of the man in Nigeria?'

'Madam, it is better to track the one in this country. In Nigeria, these people are very powerful, they make people disappear. You must help to catch them and punish them.' The next minute he moved so near to Coretta that she could smell his sour breath. 'If you catch them, please don't bring Blessing's baby o. You can see my sister. She cannot look after any baby as she is. I cannot look after any baby. Don't bring that bastard baby here. We don't even know the father. Okay? I have given you a name. Thank you very much, madam.'

He led her out of the flat and escorted her to her car.

'Give me the address of that person in Nigeria. If I have both it might help me,' said Coretta.

'I don't know it anymore, Aunty. And I will tell you something. Don't think about going to Nigeria to pursue these people. It is their territory. They can make even the President of Nigeria disappear in that country if they want. They are very powerful. Even white police cannot catch them. See that boy they killed? No head, no hands, no legs. Did police catch them? No. Do not try to catch them in Nigeria. They will kill you. Bye bye, madam.'

Twelve

Toks was finally back home in Dagenham, in bed and relieved to leave the station behind for the night. She dreaded tomorrow. It would be another gruelling day.

She dialled her father and he picked up the call on the first ring. She was happy.

'How are you, Dad?' She had the phone held close to her ear while she laid back on her pillow. She always enjoyed her evening calls to him.

'Fine, my dear girl. Are you enjoying the change in duties? No more uniform.'

'It's a bit different. More challenging. I'm looking forward to spending time with you when you come.'

'Me too! You know how tiring it can be here. We've had no electricity for months. I look forward to a break from noisy generators.'

He chuckled. Her father always ranted about Nigeria but she had made offers for him to relocate several times and he had refused. Not that she would want her mother constantly nearby.

'How about Mum?' She knew her voice sounded false and strained. If there was a way to divorce a parent, then she would have done it long ago.

'She went to see your Aunty Agnes in Ibadan.'

'Oh. I hope you are being well looked after.'

'Femi came to visit the other day.' Her father neatly changed the subject by bringing up Bode's dad. Toks was taken aback. Femi was coming up far too often for her liking.

'Bode's asking to see him.'

'Dear girl, it means that it's time. Let the boy know who his father is.'

She was silent.

'You're quiet.' Her dad knew her too well. 'He is doing very well here. He's on the presidential team.'

'That doesn't mean anything, Dad.'

'You should give him a chance, first. He should be in London in a few days. When he calls the next time, let them meet. It's time, Toks.'

'Yes, Dad.'

'It is the thing to do. You know it is. But how is your case going?'

'It's ok. A bit slow.'

'I know you can't say much but it looks dirty to me. Our big men are into occultism so I won't be surprised if someone dared to take it to England. It's happened before. Be very careful. I am happy you work with the British police. They will look after you.'

'Dad,' she said, changing the subject, 'is there news on

those ritual killers caught in the East?'

'Oh, yes. They'll definitely be hanging. The police have found 30 bodies so far. And another man just recently sacrificed one of his 13 children. He had no remorse—told the police that if the rest of the family had to have a good life, then it would involve the sacrifice of one. Life is too cheap here!' he said, resigned.

'Yes, it is.'

'Your mum said she has not heard from you.'

'Tell her I will call her later.' Toks knew she was telling a fib. She would not call her mum. They always clashed.

'Be sure to call her,' he warned. He knew her very well.

'How is Akin?' Her brother was a bone of contention. He was a wealthy businessman and a staunch supporter of native worship practices. He called himself an Africanist.

'He's fine. Doing very well. How is Coretta?'

'She's fine, Dad.'

'Her sister is doing very good work here. You all should visit. This country needs more like you.'

'Dad, it's not our fault. Tell all your contemporaries from the 60s who refuse to leave and let us 'young ones' take over. We'll turn the country around. They keep coming back to rule over and over again; they are destroying the country.'

'Hmmm.' That was her father refusing to be drawn into more talks of Nigerian government. 'There are a lot of young ones using technology to change things. It is not all that bad.'

'I know, but imagine if technology was taught to all the young ones in the whole country. Anyway, bye Dad. We'll talk later.'

'Bye, dear.'

She put the phone down.

***

At 8am sharp the next day, Toks and the team sat in the small incident room at the station and listened to Philip Dean speak.

'Katharine and Pete have done very well here. We've narrowed the core suspect families in Little Eva's investigation to 50,' he said as he looked down at their assembled faces.

'We made lots of our enquiries in local communities, including churches—thank you DC March and DC Woseley,' he said to Rose March, a small, dark and smart northern girl, and Alex Woseley, tall, bright and earnest. They had been behind the scenes doing the research.

'We're tightly focused on Black families with children aged about 4 to 6 years. We are also looking for any association to Alpha's cold case.' Philip's eyes rested on visiting Sergeant Gibbins, a heavy-set officer with a bulbous nose, who had been part of the investigating team for the torso in the Thames. DCI Jackson had brought him in to tell them more about that investigation.

'Have you ruled out copycat killing? We don't want to be after certain members of a community without a just cause. It might smack of persecution,' said DCI Jackson.

'We ruled that out. Rothman says the cut is not the same as that of the torso but must be part of a ritual. We've eliminated those in prison connected with the boy and closely questioned the groups mentioned.'

Their expression was sober as they thought of Alpha.

'Adrian, is there anything more you can tell us that would help us further?' Philip turned to DS Gibbins.

The detective shrugged his enormous shoulders. 'It remains unsolved, as you know.' DS Gibbins' voice was low and growly. It matched his girth. 'It's a case that still baffles us. I'll tell you information that never left our team.'

He saw that he had captured their attention.

'We're looking at a killer, or killers, unlike any I've ever come across. Some strange happenings went on. Most especially those that travelled to Nigeria. Now, I don't believe in anything I can't see. I don't believe that there are ghosts, demons or any such, but I don't know if I can keep to that anymore.'

Toks watched the struggle of emotions flashing across his face. He looked partly embarrassed and partly scared. He brought out a large white handkerchief from his trouser pocket and with shaking hands wiped beads of sweat off his face. All eyes were on him.

'We all, at one time or the other, were seeing something or someone that we could not explain. It was Daniel Jones,' he turned to Philip, 'you know Jones don't you? He was the first person to see the thing. Like an apparition. No bigger than a child, black as soot, sitting at the end of his bed, watching him. Daniel's like me. He's not fanciful or any such. He thought one of us was playing a trick on him. He leapt off his bed and right before his eyes the thing just faded away.'

As Toks listened to his trembling voice, her stomach lurched and she muttered a prayer under her breath.

He continued. 'We all laughed at him. Daniel loves his drink. Why not? Then I saw it too. Just like he described. It was all very strange. Grown men were reporting seeing things that shouldn't be there. We kept it between us. Except for today. And it stays that way.' He looked at them one at a time. His look was defiant as he sat back. 'We had no evidence. I wish your team good luck.'

Katherine's eyes were shining with an icy fire as she pinned him down. 'And *what* exactly did *you* see, Adrian?'

He looked anguished. 'I saw my daughter, Tanya, being led to a place and someone butchering her. That creature sat there and looked at me and like a vision I could see my Tanya with her throat cut strung upside down and her blood draining into a basin.'

He stared at the table. 'I don't believe in mumbo-jumbo, but I didn't dream about what happened to Tanya. I saw it just as clear as I'm looking at you. When we got back home to the UK I asked to be taken off the case.' He stood up. 'Many thanks for inviting me to talk.' He waved at them and quietly left the room.

There was a few second's silence as they all stared at one another. Roly Poly's shoulders started quaking with laughter as he slapped his thigh and banged the table.

'Bollocks! Rubbish!' He looked round the table and met Philip's eyes. 'Please tell me you don't believe that.'

'Pete. I don't want what we just heard to leave this room. You understand that,' said Philip.

Roly Poly's face turned surly. 'Of course. As long as you don't expect me to believe those fucking lies. You know Gibbins is on medical retirement. He went off the rails.'

'I reserve my judgement on this but we know what we have to do now. We will start questioning those families.'

Toks felt she needed time to absorb everything she had just heard. She noticed Philip and Katherine eyeing each other. There always seemed to be tension between them. Once the meeting finished, she went back to attack her paper-strewn desk. To think that a few weeks back she was lamenting the fact that she had no real detective work, and now she was so busy that she had a backlog.

***

Philip watched Katherine's eyes follow Tok's retreating back.

'Is she any good?'

'Who?'

'Don't play games with me. Your *trainee*. You seem to have taken over.'

'Yes. Very good.' He made to walk away but she pulled him back. He looked irritated.

'How are you, Philip?'

'Very well. Thanks.'

'We both know that Gibbins is telling the truth. Right? There's some black magic involved in this.' She looked him up and down, taking in his dishevelled look. 'Do you want to come over to mine later? A drink in remembrance of old times?'

'No, thanks. Some other time. It's all work for now, I'm afraid.' He pulled his arm away.

'You're such a cold arse, Philip,' she said to his retreating back. 'Do you sleep on blocks of ice?'

As Philip got to the door his phone rang. She watched his expression become sombre as he listened and then cut the call. He turned to her. 'A park in Stoke Newington. Someone just found body parts in a clay pot.'

Thirteen

Vivaldi's in Bond Street looked to Coretta like an Aladdin's cave of over-priced shoes. She eyed her sister with impatience as Melissa flitted from one elegant high heeled sandal to the next. She was on a visit to London from Nigeria and, as always, could never make up her mind about what she wanted. She had also dragged Coretta and her mum with her.

'Are you going to help her, Mum?' asked Coretta.

Their mum smiled with a twinkle in her eyes. Coretta grinned. Mum was the most laid-back person she'd ever known. In fact, she always wondered how she'd survived three high-spirited daughters. Now their mother watched fondly as Melissa tried on another pair, then slid her own dainty feet into a pair of sparkling blue sandals. 'That's nice, Mum,' said Coretta.

'No, way, Etta.' Her mother said drily as she took the shoes off. Except for her caramel colour against her mother's white one, Coretta looked quite like her mother and that pleased her. She admired her tiny waist and dark hair and hoped she would look like that at 61.

'Melissa, that pink is perfect. Go for it,' said their mum.

'You think?' Melissa eyed the shoes on her feet. They did suit her. Melissa and Katie, their other sister, took more of their physical looks from their dad. They were both tall, curvy girls. Melissa looked sensual in her tight cream T-shirt, white jeans and jacket. She had met and fallen in love with her husband Tosin when they were at university, and married him two years after they graduated. She had agonised over moving to Nigeria, but Tosin was the first son of a wealthy billionaire and had to go home and help in his father's business. Coretta had felt sorry for her sister because theirs was a close-knit family and her parents had been really upset. Especially as some parts of Nigeria were considered to be very dangerous. Twelve years later, everybody had accepted the fact that Lagos was Melissa's home. She was very happy and had two children, Coretta's nephew and niece, TJ(Tosin Junior) and Juanita. TJ had started boarding school somewhere in Suffolk and Melissa and Tosin travelled regularly to see him.

'Okay.' Melissa's long braids swung round her smooth face as she turned to the sales assistant. 'I will take these.' She had picked seven pairs.

'Great!' Coretta rubbed her growling belly, 'now we can go and eat something.'

'Aren't you getting anything?' Melissa asked Coretta. 'My treat.'

Coretta shook her head. Shopping bored her and she had enough shoes. 'No, thanks.'

'How about you Mum? That sandal was nice on you,' said

Melissa.

'Thanks, darling. Some other time.'

Coretta was fascinated by her parent's relationship. They matched so well, and loved each other very much. Perhaps it was their example that she tried to emulate with Richard.

The shop assistant took the shoes away and Melissa followed close behind her to pay.

Coretta wondered if she could get any help from her sister regarding her investigation. She had gone to the church to find Osasco, the man that Victor had mentioned. It had been hard to remove the image of Victor's sister from her mind. If the women they smuggled into the country were giving birth, what was happening to those babies? Surely the system should be able to pick something up. At the white garment church, a woman she had asked had pointed her to a man with bare feet wearing a long white gown. It was the start of the church service and the members in their white gowns, worn over their normal clothes, were trooping in. Coretta watched the man that was supposed to be Osasco talking animatedly to a short, roundish man also wearing a white gown. She decided not to approach him this time. Now that she knew where he worshipped she would go back once she had a plan. She left the premises before the man noticed.

Melissa came back laden with shopping bags.

'Here, give me those two,' said Coretta. She took some bags off her sister and they made their way to a nearby café.

It was a cute café with pink and white lace décor that made it look like an old-fashioned tea house. The girl behind the counter looked like a maid out of Downton Abbey. Cafes come and go and she wondered how long this one would last in this expensive corner of West London. Coretta happily ordered a fat veggie sandwich and a latte. Her mother ordered soup and tea and Melissa went for an Americano. Once they settled into the delicate white chairs, Melissa eyed them expectantly.

'When is my family visiting? Mum? You should come and relax in Lagos. You all work too hard here.'

'Depends on your father, dear.'

Melissa wrinkled her nose. 'You know if we left it up to him he would never come. Why don't you and Dad come over for Christmas? You'd enjoy it. It's too cold here anyway.'

Her mum put her tiny hands on Melissa's. 'It's a good idea. We'll see.'

Melissa nodded, satisfied for now. Coretta knew she would get her way and drag their parents away for Christmas. It meant she would be stuck with Richard's parents. The thought was unpalatable.

'Melissa, if you drag Mum and Dad away what would happen to myself and Katie? We need them for Christmas!'

Melissa smirked at Coretta. 'Then you should all come. We'll have a large family Christmas.'

'I'm coming soon, anyway.' Coretta let that slip casually. Sister and mother turned their full attention to her.

'Oh?' said Melissa.

'I need a bit of a break from here. I thought I could come and relax with you.'

'Coretta, come out with it. You'd never come just like that.

What do you want in Nigeria?'

She decided to come clean. 'I'm working on something. I promise it's fine. I won't cause you any trouble,' she said quickly when she saw Melissa's eyes widen.

'I hope it's not dangerous, dear,' said their mum. 'Your work scares me sometimes. You know that.' She saw Coretta's frown. 'I know you've won lots of prizes, but your...' she protested. 'And Nigeria...'

'What about Nigeria?' challenged Melissa.

Their mother turned to her. 'You know that Nigeria is not as safe as it could be... I worry about you and Tosin all the time. And now you say he wants to go into politics. That sounds even more dangerous to me. There's been so many assassinations lately.'

Melissa's face grew mutinous and Coretta squared her shoulders. Her mum had stepped into an old territory and her sister was ready for a fight.

'Mum, I love you very much. You know that. But with due respect, I would rather stay in Nigeria than here. I love it there. And yes, some parts can be dangerous as you call it because of the kidnappers, but it's not that safe here either. Nigeria is home. Mum, you know this. Tosin will be fine. We have round-the-clock protection. We can afford it. Our life there is good. I cannot exchange it for this,' she looked around disdainfully and turned to Coretta. 'You're welcome anytime you want to come, as long as you promise you're not going to get us in trouble again. Remember last time!'

She looked pensive. 'The thing I miss the most over there

is all of you.'

Her mum looked sad and Coretta felt for her. She held her mum's hand and was pleased to get a grateful smile. 'Melissa, don't forget Dad loves it here,' said Coretta.

'He's a coconut! The only Black man I know who is white,' retorted Melissa. She looked guilty at their mum's stricken look. 'I'm sorry, Mum.'

Coretta bit her lip and looked at her sister in vexation. Melissa went too far sometimes. She decided to force a change of subject as she saw something that could distract their mum.

'Mum, look! It's that TV garden guy.' They all looked up and their mum's eyes lit up when she saw the celebrity strutting into the café. This was her parent's world, so how dare Melissa try to enforce a change?

Fourteen

Toks' impression of Venue Park was a sprawling place of tall trees, bushes and grass that would have attracted a lot of families during the summer. In the winter it was dead, except for people walking their dogs and brave teenagers trying to make out in the icy weather. Today, it was alive with police and flashing lights. She and Philip approached a uniformed officer manning the gate that barred the park. Philip showed his card and the Constable nodded.

'It's right in the middle, sir. Follow that path,' he pointed.

They pushed forward with heads bent against the night drizzle that fell like mist from the moonless sky. Raindrops from the leaves trailed wet marks on their cheeks and Toks was relieved to hear voices in the distance. She only raised her head when they got louder. They arrived at a clearing surrounded by bright lights that cast huge shadows on the police officers standing by a small taped off area. Her eyes were drawn to the shrub in the middle of the scene. A police woman joined them and she recognised Mary Clark from her old unit.

'Hello Mary! What's going on here?' she asked.

Toks remembered Mary as a big Irish brunette who liked to be in the thick of the action. Mary tried to smile and failed. Toks noted the shock in her eyes and the paleness of her face.

'Toks! I heard you abandoned uniform.' Her jocular tone sounded false as she glanced at Philip. She gestured at the shrub. 'You must take a look for yourself. Here. You need these.'

She passed both of them some protective clothing.

Philip said nothing but his eyes, like Toks, were glued to the shrub. He turned to Mary. 'Has the pathologist been yet?'

'No. We're waiting for her. SOCO have been working for a while now, though.'

Philip joined the officers and began talking to them.

She lingered by Mary. 'Is it very bad?' The woman nodded as her eyes filled with tears.

Toks went to join Philip. He pulled up the tape and they both went under it. Her heart beat so loudly that all other sounds became muffled. She was right to feel as she did. They were now standing by the patch. It had close-clustered leaves with thin, scraggly branches. The earth around it was dark and wet and just by one of the low branches sat a black clay pot. She bent down beside Philip and it took a while for her brain to register what she was seeing. Then she found herself choking back bile. She could make out some reddish-yellow liquid, floating pieces of food, and at its centre nestled what looked like a child's shrivelled feet. She counted ten toes and as she peered closer, recognised some cowrie shells as well. She turned to Philip knowing her face could not hide her terror.

'What is this?' she asked.

'It's either Little Eva, or another dead or maimed child out there,' he said, and shook his head. 'What kind of animal would make a child suffer this way?'

'I don't understand it.' Tok's voice was shaky.

He looked at her intently.

'Do you recognise anything that will help us?' His voice became urgent. 'I've seen a lot of... so-called satanic cults, witch's covens... but, what is this? Is it African? Toks, please. Think!'

They looked up as they heard voices close to them. DCI Jackson, DSupt Amos and Dr Rothman walked through. Philip walked to them and Toks listened to their low conversation. Philip quickly updated them and Toks saw DSupt Amos nodding gravely. They all walked towards her. Amos and DCI Jackson nodded at her but their eyes were fixed on the pot. She stepped back and Amos pulled his sharply creased trousers up and smoothly bent down to have a look. DCI Jackson, who did the same thing, looked like he was haunching to defecate, as his trousers pulled tightly against his ample thighs. They stared.

DCI Jackson looked straight up at her, his face reddened with rage.

'Bastards! To a little child as well! Ade, do you understand any of this?' he barked at her. She did not know what to say. Yes and No?

They stood up and made way for Rothman.

She looked cool and efficient. Her sharp face softened by

make-up. Toks imagined she had come straight from another evening do.

She looked at the busy scene of crime officers in their protective gear as they started to comb the area. 'I'm happy SOCO are here. Too many people.'

She bent and set about examining the pot and its content. She pulled on her gloves and picked up each object, including the feet. Toks could see something dark, jagged and bony protruding from it and realised it was the ankle bone.

Rothman sighed. 'I can't tell you anything till I get back to the lab. DNA will tell us.' She turned her face away. 'We might be lucky this time and find more in this mishmash than we've had so far.' She swung her head at the white suited Scene Of Crime Officers who were systematically combing the ground. 'Hopefully, they'll find something.'

Philip and Toks went back to his car.

'It's a ritual sacrifice,' she said quietly. 'A lot of tribes in Nigeria still practise it but with animals. Only a hidden few do human sacrifice. Human parts are the most desired ones for money sacrifice. And there are a lot of powerful people who would do anything for money.'

'Thanks, Toks. I'm sorry I put you on the spot there. It's not up to you to know about all of this, but we need to know where it's coming from.'

'My brother does worship like this. He calls himself an Africanist. They use animals. It is the extreme ones—the ones deep in occult—that use human sacrifice. The problem is it's becoming commonplace in Nigeria. People are desperate for money.'

They arrived at the station and saw Katherine waiting at the front. As soon as she saw them she came to the car.

She didn't even acknowledge Toks, who watched them. Their heads came together. Toks could still hear them.

'It's Emily. Something happened. They refused to tell me.'

Emily? she thought. *His sister.*

He gripped Katherine's wrist before looking in Toks' direction and letting go. Katherine made her excuses and left.

'I have to go,' he said. 'It's my sister. Do as much as you can. I'll be back soon.' He re-entered the car and drove off.

***

Coretta had enjoyed her time with her mother and sister, but was relieved to continue her work on her investigation. She had arranged another meeting with Victor Essam at a Camberwell restaurant. It was a small space with a counter and basic table and chairs lined against the wall. It's pungent smell reminded her of her dad's pepper soup that he made whenever he had a cold. She remembered Melissa's outburst. Coconut indeed! The old man had taught her to cook lots of Nigerian dishes, but she was just not much into cooking. Victor sipped his Guinness as he waited for her to speak. She explained her plan that might allow them entry into the world his sister described and saw the panic appear on his face. She had slyly allowed him to enjoy half the large bottle of Guinness before presenting the idea. Now, she sipped her glass of orange juice and waited for his response

'Aunty… it's difficult work for me. Very dangerous,' he stammered.

Despite the fact that she had told him to call her Coretta, he had shifted from 'madam' to 'aunty'. It made her feel ancient. She knew she was asking a lot of him, but kept her voice low and soft. 'Victor, do these people know you?'

His face glistened with sweat as he bit his lip. 'No, but…'

'Then, all you need to do is approach one of them like a client and tell him you need a woman. Think what they did to your sister. Both of you are suffering. You found this address that we suspect might be the one your sister is talking about. Let us go in and see.'

He bit his lower lip with those teeth as she pushed.

'In terms of your status… you say your papers are nearly all sorted. It's time we get rid of people like this. Your sister escaped, but there are many more still trapped. I need the address of the warehouse in Hackney. They might be keeping children there. Who knows what might be going on?' Coretta made her voice as impassioned as possible. This was her only avenue now. 'I'll pay you what I can. I know what I'm asking you to do is dangerous, but something has to be done and we are in the position to do it.'

'Aunty, why don't we tell the police? Let us give them the information we already have.' He was more intelligent than Coretta gave him credit for.

'We don't have enough evidence, and you know I can't mention you and your sister. If we have proof, the police can catch these people. Try to take some pictures if you can. It will help.'

She watched as he bit his lip even more deeply, but his eyes shone now. Avenging his sister might help him as well.

'I will do it, Aunty. These people don't know me. Let me go see first, and we can take information to the police after this.'

Coretta opened her bag and dug for some notes. 'Here is some money. For the things you need to pay for.' What he would need to pay for was left unsaid between them.

She hoped she was close to a break. This could be her contribution to stopping the horrific use of people if she could crack it.

Victor leaned closer as some clients arguing noisily in an African language came to sit at the table next to them. One of them, completely bald, continually eyed her and licked his lips. Coretta was ready to leave the restaurant.

'Aunty, you know that last time we spoke—did I tell you that one of Osasco's women is in prison here?' Coretta's heart lifted. Her breakthrough might be more than one. 'Her name is Ukeria. They catch her for drugs. She is there suffering and didn't name anyone because they say that Osasco is looking after her children and family back home in Nigeria. I don't know if you will get anything from her if you go to see her.'

'Which prison?'

'They say Wandsworth. Ukeria... hmmm,' he looked upward and closed his eyes. 'I think her other name is Imafidon. Maybe she will help you, maybe she will not. You can try her.' He looked anxious again. 'I will call you back in a few days and let you know how far I get.'

It could be a fantastic development if Victor got more information for them. She stood up and avoided looking at the staring balding man. Next time she would ask them to meet in another restaurant. This one with its shady clientele gave her the creeps.

Fifteen

Philip was at the hospital. He stood and watched Emily's tightly scrunched eyes. Her paper-thin skin was nearly as white as the pillow covers she was lying on. He knew she was not asleep. He walked to the chair at the side of the bed and sat.

'Emily,' he called softly. Her eyelids flickered but she kept them shut. 'Emily.' Her eyes slowly opened. She still seemed a bit dazed.

'How're you feeling?'

She said nothing but lifted both arms that had been lying still beside her. He saw the bandages that covered them from her shoulders down to her wrists. The home's service manager had told Philip what had happened in sober, apologetic tones. It was all he could do not to punch the man's trembling lips. He was at least a head taller than Philip with a powerfully built body, but he knew he could have felled him with a single blow.

'How did she overdose on her medication? What did she use to cut her arms like that?' he asked.

'We're still investigating, I'm afraid. We do regular checks to ensure that things like this don't happen.'

'But it has,' he replied tightly. 'This is downright negligence.'

'We have done continuous assessment on her and she has never presented this kind of issue. I mean, she was very happy when her friend came to visit.' He was wringing his hands now.

'Her friend?' Philip asked.

'Yes. Her friend. We were glad that she could have company. They chatted and had strolls round the garden. It was quite unlike Emily, I must say.'

'Can you remember this friend's name?'

The man shook his head. 'I will need to check the visitor's books. She had had visitors in the beginning who had been cleared by you, but they stopped coming over the years. This is one of the visitors that used to visit her earlier.'

Austin. He hoped it was not Austin. What would he want with Emily after all these years? He used to visit Emily in the early days but stopped. It was a great relief when he disappeared. The Manager went to get his book and confirmed that it was him. Philip did not know what Austin wanted, but knew what damage he had done in the past.

'Please do not allow her anymore visitors unless they've been cleared through me. She's too vulnerable. Meanwhile, I'm going to make a formal complaint regarding what happened to my sister here.'

He gazed at Emily's reddened eyes, then held her hand. She tried to prise it free. He did not let go. He would track

Austin down. The address he had written in the hostel visitor's book could be fake, but he would start from there. Philip knew of one other person who might know about this. *Katherine.*

***

The next few days had been busy for the team, between Venus' stonewalled investigation and Little Eva's sprawling one, so Toks was surprised to see DCI Jackson in front of his cubicle gesturing to her as she entered the squad room. She sighed inwardly. He had been unhappy with all of the media drama around the latest find. Toks followed him into his office and he indicated the chair across from his small, tidy desk. There was a photo of his Dominican wife, his mixed-raced daughter and son, and a grandchild. It was fascinating. His wife was all smiles with her head tilted back and a look of pleasure as she stared straight at the camera. They were said to have been happily married for 35 years. Lucky him. There was an impatient rustling of papers and she quickly turned back to him. He shoved them across to her.

'I don't know how this shit happened, Ade.'

She scanned the headlines on the sheaf of papers he gave her: 'Clay pot sacrifice' was splashed across one. 'African *juju* in a London park,' screamed another. The press had not been allowed access to pictures but someone from the department had leaked information to them. Toks looked at another paper. There was a sketch of the pot with all that had been found in it. It made her feel sick all over again. She knew that he was watching her but deliberately made her face expressionless.

'Dean said you might know a little about this *juju* business. We need to track down someone who can tell us more.'

'Sir, beyond knowing that this could be human sacrifice, I can't say much more,' she said carefully, and avoided looking at the sketch again. Roly Poly had started cracking loud crude jokes about Africans and parks. She had ignored him because if she made a big issue it could escalate.

'Superintendent Amos has another press conference this morning. They're on us to solve this quickly.' His phone rang. 'I've got to take this,' he said.

She left. Things were starting to get more complicated with no end in sight. The only thing that made Toks slightly happy at the moment was that she was visiting Coretta and Richard soon. At least that was something to look forward to. She checked her watch. She was due to meet Philip in the morgue to see Dr Rothman. He was already there, looking drawn and red-eyed. She wondered if it was because of his sister. Her stomach churned as the cold odour of the morgue swamped her nose. Toks felt Katherine's hard eyes on her and ignored it. Dr Rothman had x-rays up on the board, and matter from the clay pot laid out on plastic sheets on a trolley.

'It's highly likely that these came from the same child. DNA will definitely tell us. The same type of weapon that was used to cut the hand also cut these.'

Toks looked at the almost-black, bloodied stumps that Rothman had laid on a second trolley. 'The cuts were post-mortem. The child was already dead when they were made.

It accounts for much less blood than there should have been otherwise. If you look closely around the ankles...' Toks saw Katherine angling forward eagerly, '...you can see that it is not a clean cut. At least 3 or 4 chops before the ankles were detached from the body. The food objects that were placed in the pot do not have any meaning for me, but we're analysing everything found and the composition of the pot itself might give us some answers.'

'I can help you identify some of them,' Toks said.

Dr Rothman smiled at her for the first time. 'Thanks, DC Ade. That would be really helpful.'

Sixteen

Victor was afraid. This was a very difficult thing that Aunty had asked him to do. But he took a deep breath and thought about his sister sitting and waiting in the darkness of his living room. He was standing in front of a house in Brixton. He looked around cautiously as the freezing, sharp air steamed his breath. The street was small like his own and the houses, tiny. Cars of different types lined it bumper to bumper. He raised his hand to knock on the door and realised that someone was already opening it. The man standing before him was a bit taller than him, with an open, smiling face. Victor noticed that most of his teeth were brown and crooked.

'I saw you standing there. Come in, come in.' Victor hesitated then entered. The man turned and led him into a small lounge.

He tried not to shiver as he imagined his sister in this house. He prayed he would be able to leave the place with something that would help Aunty go to the police. Something that would allow him and his sister to be free again.

'Sit down,' the man gestured to a comfortable, wine leather

chair. 'You want drink? I have brandy, vodka, Guinness… eh?'

'Nothing.' Victor saw the smile slipping and hastily added, 'Okay… maybe Guinness.'

'Good, good…' Victor wondered why the house was so quiet. Was he being led into a trap? The man brought a bottle of Guinness, a glass and an opener, which he placed on a stool in front of Victor.

'I will add the money to your bill at the end eh? I will take £100 + £10 for the drink. When the lady come,' his smile became a leer, 'you will know it is worth it. She is a sweet lady, o. Trust me.' He gave Victor a broad wink. 'She know how to do the business. Anything you ask her, she do for you.' His eyes became dreamy and he unconsciously rubbed the front of his trouser. 'You will enjoy this evening my brother, and you will come back again… your madam at home will not perform like this girl. Let me go and call her.' He left the room.

Victor felt bad when he realised that this must be what his sister went through. He heard low voices at the door. The man came in first, followed by a short, shapely woman.

'Here she is… her name is Helena. She will look after you well. I will leave you and come back later. She will take you to her room eh. Helena, look after this man very well o.' He winked at Victor and left them.

Helena moved to Victor and sat on his lap. She was pretty, with full lips and long wavy extensions tumbling down her shoulders. He felt her soft body through a short, silky night gown that barely covered her bum and exposed her huge cleavage. She pulled his face to her neck and his nose filled with her perfumed smell. Victor tried to push her hands away but he found himself unable to. She took his hands and placed them on her breasts. He heard her moaning softly. This wasn't how he'd planned it. He made to push her away, but instead heard himself saying, 'Can we go to your room?'

'I will take you…' Her voice was soft. The palm of her hand as she pulled him out of the room was soft. He felt drawn. She led him through the dark hallway into a large room dominated by a king-sized bed. The curtains were drawn and a little lamp in the corner was their only illumination. He could smell her musky odour in this room. She drew him to the bed, made him lie down and sat on top, facing him. She pulled the thin straps of her gown off her shoulder and pressed his face to her chest. He felt himself go stiff and decided to pull away. *It will not happen!* He tried to think more clearly as she ground her body against his trousers and attempted to take off his belt.

'I will pleasure you so well tonight,' she whispered softly into his ear as her busy hands worked at his belt.

'Are they keeping you prisoner here?' he whispered softly, and felt her go rigid. She freed the belt and plunged her hands down his trousers. 'You have to let me know. I can help you,' Victor gasped.

She put her mouth close to his ears. 'We must continue… There're cameras… They sell my action as well. If I don't do it with you tonight, I'm in trouble.' She pulled down his trousers and quickly produced a condom from her robe. She expertly sheathed him and then arched her body. He felt himself shuddering. It was too much. He heard his own distant moan.

***

'Where is Austin?' Philip asked Katherine. He had asked to have a quick chat with her at the King Richard pub near the station. She gave him a sardonic smile. She was wearing a dress that showed off her full figure and he knew the men around would be watching their table like hounds.

'How would I know? I haven't seen him in years.'

'Katherine. This is a serious matter. Emily harmed herself. It happened after Austin visited her.'

She looked surprised. 'Austin visited Emily?'

'You and she were best friends once. I'm appealing to that friendship now. You need to tell me where Austin is. '

Her raised palms stopped him. She looked around them. Then leaning across the table said, 'You chose the wrong place to come and have this conversation. What did you think? That I would eat you? All eyes are on us. I'll tell you this once, so that you understand it. The minute Emily threw in her lot with Austin she lost my friendship. You wrapped your life around her's and see how you've suffered for it. Emily swung to the dark side. Austin practised Satanism and Satanists have no loyalty to anyone but themselves and their master. She's lost.'

'Forget Austin and support Emily as best as you can.'

Philip said nothing.

'You've got that Sphinx expression on your face again. I'm serious. Move on from this. Pick up your life again. You should be where Jackson is, or Amos! You've turned down enough promotions as it is. Your continuing to be a Sergeant is beyond a joke now.'

He wanted to walk out of the room. He didn't need career counselling from Katherine. He needed to help Emily.

She stood up. 'Sorry I can't help you. See you at the briefing tomorrow.'

Seventeen

After the team brief the next day, Philip, Toks and Katharine were back at the morgue at Dr Rothman's request. Toks watched as the pathologist's eyes followed Philip and Katherine's whispered conversation with a slight upturn of her lips. It would have been great to know what she was thinking. Katherine caught the doctor's look and eyed her in return. All around them hung the still enlarged photographs of the black clay pot, whilst a long metal table held labelled plastic containers.

'DNA results confirm that this is the same child. We also know it is a she. Thanks to Toks, we were able to identify all the contents of the pot.' She pointed to pictures of the lumpy matter that Toks had recognised and identified to her as yam, and then walked to the table and picked up a container. She opened it. 'This is plantain, and the reddish liquid that covered everything is known as palm oil.' She pointed to the picture of a small keg filled with palm oil. 'Palm oil is from the fruit of the oil palm tree and is an important ingredient in soap and such products. It is unsaturated fat and solidifies on contact with cold air or water, hence the waxy look. Most importantly, palm oil is used to cook a variety of sauces and food in Africa, especially West Africa. The food was placed around her feet before being drenched in it.' She rested her eyes on Philip. 'What all this means, I cannot tell, so I suggest you get an expert. It does look like ritual sacrifice and it could be West African in origin. Curiously though, there was hardly any blood. We know she was dead before all this happened, but even then, it looked like blood drained from the feet, and the only way that can happen is if the body was hung upside-down like is done with animals in a slaughterhouse.'

There was silence. Toks thought of Gibbins' vision of his daughter and shivered.

****

Coretta always felt depersonalised when she visited prisons. At Wandsworth prison, her ID was checked, her belts, phones and anything that could be deemed harmful to a prisoner collected before she went through the scanner. Another beep. *Just like an airport.*

She had been a regular here when she was writing a book on drug mules. A female warden with a grim face, bumpy with acne, led her to the visitor's room and she waited for Ukeria Imafidon to be brought in. Several other wardens sat at a table and chatted away after briefly glancing her way. The door opened and a stout woman wearing grey jogging bottoms and a loose baggy top that could not hide her bulges was led in. She had a mound of a stomach, large hips and a generous chest.

'You've only got half an hour,' said the warden with the acne.

She watched them with unfriendly eyes before joining her colleagues. Coretta regretted that her prison contact, Mabel, was not on duty. She faced her 'guest'.

'I'm Coretta Davies.'

'Hello madam Coretta,' mumbled Ukeria.

'I'm a writer and I'm working on an investigation that I hope you might be able to help me with.'

'What investigation?' She suddenly came back to life and looked nervous. 'You did not tell me that on the phone. Why did you tell me that you're from the church?' She stood up. 'I don't want to deal with a liar.'

Coretta paused. She needed answers from this woman. It was very important not to scare her, but she had only half an hour and sometimes direct tactics worked better than a softer approach.

'Sit down, I will explain.'

The woman reluctantly sat down and crossed her plump arms across her chest, staring crossly at Coretta.

'I want to travel to Nigeria. I hear that most of the child smuggling rings are controlled from there and that you might know something about it.'

'Why should I know? Didn't they tell you what I come in for? Not for child smuggling. You have the wrong person.' She made to stand up again and Coretta, noting the warden turning in their direction, moved nearer and lowered her voice. The proximity filled her nose with the stench of sweat, but it was important for her to leave the place with answers.

'Wait… I can make this worth your while. I need some answers.'

The woman sat down and leaned forward. '£5,000,' she whispered in a firm voice.

'You don't even know what I want to ask you.'

'I already know. It's about the boy. You're not the only one come to visit. They all want the story and yet they don't understand any of it.'

'Make me understand.'

'Are you ready to give me £5,000?'

'I don't have £5,000. That's a lot of money for me.'

'Then I don't have anything to tell you.' She tried to stand up again.

'You know who smuggled the boy in? Do you know where he came from? Do you know who he is?' asked Coretta.

Ukeria sat down, eyes hard. 'I will tell you something that you people don't know. You don't understand us. What we are. You come and just take over countries and put Christianity and say, 'finish'. It's not finished.'

Coretta felt her face grow hot in anger at the lack of remorse. 'Does traditional worship involve the killing of children?'

'Look, if you want information from me, you give £5,000. I will tell you who to pay it to outside. I'm serving a jail sentence and my children at home are suffering. We have to survive. Simple.'

'So, are you telling me you approve of people sacrificing children for their gods?'

'People do what they must.'

'But why do it here in Britain? Why do it where every eye in the West is on them?'

'Because it is what will make this more powerful. Take it from me, Madam Coretta. The people that killed the boy were looking for something very big and very important in the UK. It is always all about money. Find out what it is and you will find them.'

'What can anyone want that makes them take an innocent life?'

'Pay me and I will give you a good contact in Nigeria. You will get all your answers.'

'I don't have £5,000. I can give you £3,000. Half when you tell me what I need from here, and half when I get what I need from Nigeria.'

'You think the journalists and all those people have not offered me more?' She moved her face nearer and Coretta could see the greenish hues around her forehead where the skin had been ruined from some form of chemical peeling. 'I'm talking to *you*. Not them. Will you ask me why?'

'Ok, why?'

'Because you're the only Nigerian who come to me. I know your skin is very light, but I know you come from there. You will understand the whole story. Make it £4,000.'

'No, £3,000. Now what have you got to tell me?'

The woman smiled for the first time. 'I cannot tell you like that. Somebody will call you when you leave here. You will give me your number. When she call you, you will give her the money. Cash. She will give you part of the story and the name of the person that will tell you the rest in Nigeria. When you hear the rest, you give him the other half.'

'Fine.'

Ukeria stood up and signalled to the warden who had been moving towards them anyway. Their time was up. Another warden, a man this time, led Coretta back to the reception. He looked like a convict himself with his clean-shaven head and battered face. He did not try to strike up a conversation and Coretta was glad. She had a lot to think about. It was hard to know whether she had made the right decision in that room or not. She would be parting with £3,000. At least the payment was not all at once. She might also be onto something big. She collected her things and left the prison.

***

Philip finally delivered on his word and paired Toks up with Katherine to visit Professor William White, an expert in African spiritualism and occultism. His office at the SOAS in London was crammed with academic books and journals. He was a pale, tall man with full, ink black hair and dark eyes, magnified behind black framed-glasses that reminded her of a bookish Dracula. He welcomed both of them with limp hand-shakes, then gestured for them to sit with a wave of his hand. It occurred to her that Richard, Coretta's husband, could have done this for them, as he was also an expert. The professor's eyes lingered on Katherine's face before fixing on Tok's chest. Katherine gave him an overview of the case. He pursed his lips as they showed him the crime scene photos, but his face grew animated as he examined photograph after photograph. Eventually, he reluctantly laid them on the table.

'This is not Alpha. I don't know what made any of you think it was in any way related to him.'

He started muttering under his breath, but clearly loud enough for them to hear.

'Alpha was a ritual sacrifice, his torso thrown in water. Body left in a very public place but no remains elsewhere. Meaning, the torso itself was the main sacrifice. There's great significance in throwing his body into the Thames. A cleansing sacrifice to an Orisha.' His face became grim. 'Sacrifices made in the rivers are mostly to Orishas—gods and goddesses of the river. Most of *these people* offer animal sacrifice, but human sacrifice is technically more powerful. Very prevalent in Nigeria, South Africa, Brazil. Greatest source of quick money. The more innocent the blood, the more value. Women as well, with the connection to fertility and the earth mother.'

'What does it all mean, professor?' Katherine asked. Toks detected a note of disdain in her voice and hid a smile. Besides, she was having problems with the ripe smell issuing from the room as well. The professor clearly spent a lot of time in his airless office.

He gave her an annoyed look. 'It's not an exact science. Female parts are the most lucrative to harvest. They are regarded as very potent for financial gain. The boy, to my estimation, did not fit within the profile as a sacrifice for money. He was a cleansing sacrifice. He was used to heal someone very important to them who had been extremely ill.'

Toks nodded. This gaunt academic might irritate her, but it did not stop her from being impressed. She imagined the years he must have devoted to gathering this amount of knowledge.

She decided to try and tap him for some background information. 'Professor?' The eyes moved back to her chest. 'What can you tell us about the pictures themselves?'

'The sacrifices in this picture are of a different kind. I believe they have been made to *Eshu*. It's not a cleansing sacrifice, it's an appeasing one. It means that someone venerates this god and has offered the highest of sacrifices: shedding the blood of an innocent. Some cults are known to ask their members to sacrifice their own children. *Eshu's* sacrifice is made with blood drained directly onto a black mound of earth and clay. Whoever did this sacrifice would have that mound in their home. *Eshu* sacrifice is made in various parts of Africa, but referred to by different names.'

He finally turned the thick lenses from her chest to her face.

'You do know that another name for *Eshu* is 'the little devil?" he said, with a toothy smile that was almost cute in a geeky way. 'A demon that is seen as a direct messenger to god.'

Toks shivered. She was doing a lot of that in this case. 'Thank you, Professor.' They said their goodbyes and even before they closed the door behind them he was already engrossed in a book that he had picked from under his sheaf of papers.

'So what do you think of all that?' Katherine asked Toks as they drove away from the university. 'It looks as if he's narrowed down the search to certain parts of Africa.'

'I think we might need to look at it from another angle and to be careful not to pick on groups...' Toks said.

'You mean like picking on people from certain parts of Nigeria and asking about goddesses? We can't do that anyway, rest assured,' she informed Toks carelessly. 'Besides, most Africans I have come across are Christians. What we come against mostly in our team are cases of one or two churches trying to exorcise some poor child, believing they're possessed. But, can I ask a personal question?'

Toks felt her shoulders tense. She was trapped in a car with this woman.

'Yes?'

'I know you're a Christian. How does it feel? Do you have doubts when crazy things happen?'

'You just have to have faith. Only God understands why. It's a relationship that you build with Him.'

'It seems hard to do that. I hope you don't take offence at this, but people from Africa can be very spiritual, can't they?'

Toks felt the palpable tension between them.

'I guess so,' she said.

'Most of what the professor said seems to be true,' she persisted.

'There is ritual worship in Nigeria and *all over the world*,', said Toks, not wanting to sound defensive. 'It depends on people's belief system.'

They journeyed down to the station with no more words between them. Toks was more than happy with that. She might invite Katherine to church one day.

Eighteen

At the station the next day, Toks went to get coffee and saw Katherine deftly picking a bag of crisps from the dispenser. The other woman assessed her with a smile, slightly thawed from the day before.

'You seem to have hit some note with DS Dean. You're lucky. He's a great mentor.' She walked away before Toks could reply.

Later, as they sat in the car, Philip explained the plan for the afternoon. He waved a list. 'We'll try to cover at least 3 families from this list. I think it's best to first visit the ones whose neighbour's contacted us. It was good that Amos added the whistle blowing part to his news conference. I think you called the school of the Ezogie children?' Toks nodded. A neighbour had phoned to tell them they were worried that they hadn't seen the children in this family for a while and Philip had Toks call their school. The headteacher, an abrupt sounding woman, had told her the family had been given permission to attend a funeral back in Nigeria and had returned.

'Let's check that all is well and cross them off our list. They live around Dalston area and are known to be ardent church goers.' He glanced at her.

'Does that connect to our investigation?' she asked.

'Not particularly. Be observant when we get there. They are only one of about 20 families to visit in the next few days.'

He manoeuvred the car through the busy Dalston traffic and drove to a side street lined with terraced houses and cars. He parked in a small space and turned off the engine.

They walked up to a door embossed with a gold number 28. They could hear noise within and after a few rattling of chains the door opened. Framed in the doorway was a plump man of medium height. He eyed them warily and frowned.

'Hello, how can I help you?'

'Hello, Mr Ezogie. This is detective Ade and I am detective Dean, from the police,' he said, showing his warrant card. 'May we come in?'

The man looked around the street as if expecting neighbours to be watching but all was quiet. They entered a hallway. Toks inhaled the pungent, slightly off odour of stock fish and Nigerian native soup. She knew how delicious the soup could be and it made her instantly hungry but saw the flare of DS Philip's nostrils. She would have to introduce him to Nigerian food someday.

They followed him into a front room with a gas fire and comfortable black leather chairs. 'Please sit down,' he said.

They sat. She had been looking around them with interest and could not see any sign that there were children in the house. No toys or books. Only a mirror and a painting of fruits on the wall. A fussy, starched curtain was pulled back to let in the weak winter sunshine.

He sat facing them. 'Can you tell me why you are here, please?'

'We are questioning families around the area as part of our investigation for a missing child.'

'Ok, Officer,' he acknowledged quietly. 'Our church is not far from here and some of the families have already told me. As far as I know, they said your officers have been polite and conducting things well.'

Philip nodded. 'We would not do otherwise. We don't want to intrude longer on your afternoon, but may I ask where your children are?' He brought out his notebook. 'You have Beauty and Sunday, Grace and Ogo. Three girls and a boy. But they are not at school?'

'Yes,' said Mr Ezogie. 'Their maternal grandfather died and they have gone for his funeral with their mother in Nigeria. We took appropriate permission from their school.'

'Can you tell us how old they are?'

'Beauty and Sunday are 10, twins, Ogo is 8, and Grace, 4. She will not start school till next September.'

Philip made more notes. 'Thank you. They're not back yet?'

'They missed their flight. They'll be back tomorrow.'

'Would you mind if we looked around?'

The man seemed taken aback. 'Yes, I do. We have nothing to hide, but you will need a search warrant.'

'It's not to search, just for a quick look,' Toks said.

He looked reluctant. 'I would prefer if you did not. I am not obstructing justice, but you will need a warrant.'

'That's fine,' said Philip.

'Before we go, may I please use your toilet?' Toks asked, avoiding Philip's eyes.

'That's fine, Officer,' said Mr Ezogie, looking uneasy. He knew she had somehow sidestepped him. 'Follow me.'

He pointed up a set of carpeted stairs. 'It's up there, just in front of you.'

She ensured he went back into the room before going up. She went past the toilet to a door on the left of the tiny corridor. It was a children's room—a bunk bed and a single bed. Clothes were strewn all over the carpeted floor. She left, and pushed through a second door to the right, opening the master bedroom. A king-sized bed, the same stiff curtain as the front room window, large dressing table, hair brushes, perfume bottles and various jars and tubs of makeup. A framed picture of a sophisticated looking light skinned woman, whom she took to be Mrs Ezogie, sat in the middle of the mess. Toks took a hair brush, then went back out to the tiny toilet, flushing the empty toilet to keep up pretences. She opened a white cabinet on the wall and saw some children's toothbrushes which she picked up and jammed into a small supermarket carrier bag, before pushing them deep into her coat pocket. It was all done in less than 10 minutes and she was back downstairs. Philip was already standing up while Mr Ezogie looked at her and said nothing.

'Thank you very much. We look forward to seeing your children and wife in a few days' time,' Philip said. The man nodded and escorted them to the front door.

They settled back in the car and he looked at her before starting the engine.

'They have a children's room upstairs. I took some toothbrushes and the mum's hairbrush,' she said.

'They aren't under suspicion, but we can keep them for now. We have two more families to visit around here.' She was glad he didn't tell her off for her unplanned search of the Ezogie house.

Their visits took the rest of the afternoon. One set of children had gone to visit their maternal grandparents, another set, the Ezogies, had gone for a funeral, and one set was back at school.

As he parked at the front of the station, he turned to her.

'What's your feeling about all this?'

'I'm not sure yet,' Toks said. She had not felt any alarm bells and even felt foolish with the toothbrush and hairbrush in the carrier bag.

'Let's check the hair DNA on the brush, presumably the wife's, against the toothbrushes. It might not be admissible in court, but who knows. I'll get Rothman to do it.'

Nineteen

Coretta tapped her fingers on the steering wheel as she planned the rest of her day. She was on her way to Thamesmead, South East London to meet Ukeria's sister with the £1,500. She would then visit Victor's house and find out why he was avoiding her. It seemed that particular line of investigation was now a dead-end. She looked around at the stretch of houses and new developments in the former Thamesmead marsh-lands. When she was searching for property and thinking about the cheaper end of the market, her mortgage adviser had dissuaded her from looking at this former enclave of council houses and white working class, saying that the houses might suffer from subsistence in years to come. So she had avoided it. Thamesmead was so far from Richmond it was like another world. There was a large tract of land that the local council used as borough waste grounds. But many parts of it boasted cheap and affordable houses that emerging immigrants, especially those from Africa, snapped up on their step up the property ladder. Janet, one of her old school friends who was also a property developer, said she would not touch Thamesmead with a barge pole. But Janet could speak with her multimillion-pound worth of property portfolio. It was a good thing that she and Richard were weathering the economy well, and she was thankful that she had hung onto their portfolio. It had left them with some solid properties in the Docklands. She made a left turn at a large roundabout and knew she was nearing her destination. Within minutes, her google map announced that she had arrived. There was parking right in front of the house. It was quiet but she could imagine how noisy and crowded it could get after 3pm when children got out of school. The houses on this street were identical, small brown brick buildings with varied coloured doors and small front parking areas. A red Nissan Micra was parked in front of the address that she wanted. She went to the door and pressed the bell. It opened, revealing a copy of Ukeria.

'Are you Coretta?'

'Yes. Margaret?'

'Come in,' she said, shifting her large frame to the side as Coretta squeezed through.

She led the way to her front room.

'Sit down, please.' She gestured to a dining chair. Coretta sat. The woman sat across from her. Coretta noted that the chair was too small for her big behind. Just like her sister.

'Ukeria said I should tell you everything I know. But, please give me the money first.'

Coretta delved into her bag and gave her the money. 'I need as much information as possible.'

The woman looked sceptical, which did nothing to

reassure Coretta.

'I have always told my sister that she needs to stop looking for easy ways to make money. You know why she's in jail? Drugs! I don't know what she's doing with all these bad people. Me, I came here, studied nursing, and little by little I sorted myself out. I have bought my own house, my children are in higher education, and that is the way it should be.' There was a long pause. Coretta could see intelligence, and something else, shining from her eyes. 'Ukeria said you would tell me about the boy that was thrown in the river.'

'Hmmm. Did she?'

'I need solid information that will help me here and over in Nigeria.' Coretta tried to remove the trace of impatience from her voice. She did not need anyone playing games with her. Not after £1.5k.

'You know you cannot survive there on your own with your light skin. Ukeria said you are Nigerian.'

Coretta decided it was time to put her journalistic skills to the test. Open questioning was not going to work here.

'Who were the people that brought that boy to this country?'

'Ukeria says she knows them but she does not tell me everything. She says that these people are very dangerous and very powerful. That the government here is wasting time looking at small-time smugglers, but that they can kill her if they know she spoke. Even in the jail where she is. I want to protect my sister.'

Coretta felt dissatisfied and it must have shown on her

expression as Margaret said, 'Ukeria said I should give you a book. Wait.'

Coretta rolled her eyes as the woman left the room. She had been toying with her all this while when she was meant to give her a book. Margaret came back into the room holding a small notebook.

'I hope it will give you the information you want.'

'I hope so as well,' said Coretta, as she held out her hand.

Margaret ignored the comment and continued. 'Before they sent her to jail, they raided her house and took everything there. Ukeria had already given me this book to keep. In another year, she will be a free woman. Please don't let her name appear anywhere.'

She gave the book to Coretta and then checked a watch with tiny straps on her dimpled wrist. 'I will need to go and get ready for work.'

Coretta held the book up. 'Are you sure that you have nothing else to tell me? This book looks too small for the money I just gave you.'

'My sister told me that it will give you what you want. Remember it was you that negotiated with her. She told me to collect the money and give you the book.' She walked to the door and Coretta followed her undulating bottom. 'I always tell her to be careful but she landed herself in a right mess.'

'Coretta, I know you are paying Ukeria well for what you want but I hope you heard what I said earlier. These people are very dangerous. Be careful.'

Her big frame was still silhouetted at the door when Coretta waved goodbye and entered her car. The book felt like hot coal in her bag. It was difficult to manoeuvre with Margaret's eyes on her but she did. She drove away and spotted a quiet side road and parked there. There was no way she would wait to get home before opening that book.

***

DCI Jackson bit his cheek and then wiped the back of a trembling hand across his mouth. He had suffered a mild stroke years before and in times of stress the tremor returned. He shook his head at Philip who sat across him.

'Okay Philip, run me through where we are.'

'We narrowed it down to one family and are bringing them in for questioning. They were on our original list of suspects. Ade and I visited the family about a week ago. They live in Dalston.'

'And?'

'Grace, 4, did not come back from Nigeria with the mother and another one of their children, Ogo, 8, is also missing. Their neighbour tipped us off. The father told us Grace is his daughter. The neighbour said they told her she is a niece. It's not adding up.'

'Did you find out why she's no longer with them? And where is the other daughter?'

'They claimed Grace went back to Nigeria. That was when the father started claiming his rights. We went back yesterday but found no-one at home.'

'We're still waiting for the DNA results?'

'Rothman says any day now,' said Philip.

DCI Jackson looked thoughtful. 'Are you sure of your info? Some neighbours can be malicious. And how about the 8-year-old? What was the father's explanation?'

'Said she went to visit an aunty. I feel this…' Philip's eyes were intense and his expression sharp.

This is a man that could be sitting where I'm sitting, thought DCI Jackson. A man who was known as the Razor. One that never really fit in.

'This family is hiding something,' continued Philip, aware of Jackson's study. 'If they're not, why have they disappeared? Let's track them and bring them in for questioning. We've got no other leads.'

Philip thought about Austin. He had staked out three buildings with no luck. If the one tonight didn't work, he'd have to give up. Emily's situation was not helping, as the hostel was asking for her to be rehoused. He desperately needed to find Austin.

'What's happening to the Venus case? All our men are still out there and it's gone cold. Amos is really shitting on me. We need closure.' He peered at Philip. 'I hope The Razor's still there, Philip. I need you for this.'

'Maybe we'll get something from this couple, maybe not. At least it eliminates a line of questioning,' answered Philip. 'As for Venus, Toks is continuing the background investigation alongside the manpower we have placed out there.'

'How is Ade? She any good?'

'She's sharp and keen.'

'Good recommendation there. One of the best uniforms—known to sweat the sweat with the boys. Is she gelling?'

'Yes.'

Jackson leaned forward again and his hands went out in front of him to crudely describe Tok's breasts. His breath engulfed Philip in cheese and garlic. 'Between you and me, don't let those fool you. Large enough to make a man look nowhere else, but she's tough. How about you and Katherine? Once bitten eh?' He looked at Philip's wooden face. 'We should do something together soon.'

Jackson picked up his phone and was already chatting away as Philip left the room.

***

Days later, Toks was pleased when they finally found Mr and Mrs Ezogie, hiding out with some relatives in Enfield. The interview room, with its spindly chairs, scarred table and recording equipment, was ready. They were interviewing the husband first.

Mr Ezogie, whom a week ago was cool and calm when they visited, now exuded a strong, sweaty animal smell as his eyes darted round the little space. He already looked like he would cave under questioning.

She checked her notes again. Mr and Mrs Ezogie. British naturalised Nigerians. From Edo state, Benin City. Devoted church-goers. The husband traded in African food stuff in the local market in the day time and was a leader at their church at the weekend. The wife owned a cosmetics shop in the same market. They had been married for 15 years.

'Right,' said Philip, 'we have been searching for you and your wife. Why did you leave your home with your children and move in with your relatives?'

Sweat started pouring down the man's face.

'We went to an event for our relatives,' he said. He brought out a large white handkerchief from his pocket and wiped his face with trembling hands. Toks kept thinking this was a far cry from the arrogant man that they had questioned.

'Where are Grace and Ogo?' she asked.

'Grace is back home in Nigeria. Ogo is with her Aunty in Kent.'

'You will provide us with phone numbers and addresses for us to check this,' she said.

The sweat was now in free flow and damp patches bloomed all over his rumpled linen shirt. 'It is hard to make contact with the village by phone,' said the man.

'We will still want the number and address. You said Grace is your niece. Who are her parents?'

'Grace is my wife's late sister's daughter. We brought her to the UK to bring her up as our own, but we've since sent her back to Nigeria.'

'Have you got proof of this?'

'Yes, we have.'

'We'll need a picture of Grace and her travel documents. You need to take us to Ogo, and as there is a question around the parentage of your children we will be doing a DNA test,' said Philip.

Philip gave him a piece of paper and watched as Mr Ezogie wrote down contacts for Ogo, but only an address in Nigeria for Grace.

'Please write down a phone contact for Grace,' Toks said, observing him closely. The man brought out the sodden handkerchief and wiped his face again.

'My wife has all the other details,' he said, avoiding her eyes. They escorted him out to a uniformed officer and brought in Mrs Ezogie.

She was an attractive, assured woman in her mid to late 30s. Toks attributed her glossy curls to a good hairdresser and her gold jewellery to a taste for expensive trinkets. Her skin was as light as her husband's was dark. It was definitely her picture she saw on the dresser. The woman smelled of good perfume.

They asked her the same questions and she answered confidently.

'We went to a church conference in Enfield. We had no idea that you wanted to talk to us. You will need to tell us why and we will want to consult with our lawyer,' she said.

'You may consult your lawyer but we only want to know Grace's whereabouts. We're not detaining you and you're free to leave anytime you want, although asking to speak to a lawyer could extend the time you'll stay with us,' said Toks.

The couple could still be charged, she thought, as they probably had the little girl smuggled into the country.

Philip noted that Mrs Ezogie looked less composed at that.

'We gave her to someone who took her safely back home. They assured us that she is back in the village.'

Toks said they would need to do DNA on the children and Mrs Ezogie flared up.

'Why do you need to do a DNA test? We have proof from the hospital where I had all my children! Grace is the only one that is not our child and now you know!'

'You're telling me that someone brought your niece into the country and for reasons known to you, you instructed the self-same person to send her back to your village? And you then got assurance from this person that the child is back in the village?' Toks was losing patience with the woman.

'Yes, we did.'

'Why?' Toks asked.

Mrs Ezogie stared at the table and said nothing.

'Again, I am asking for a phone number to reach Grace.'

Parroting her husband, she said it was difficult to reach people in the village and that the number had stopped working.

'In this day of WhatsApp, Messenger? I'm afraid you've landed yourself in a spot of trouble. What you've done is called child smuggling,' said Philip.

'Mrs Ezogie,' he said, 'we are arresting you for the abduction of your niece, Grace.'

Her eyes widened and she jumped up shouting, 'You tricked us! We need to speak to our lawyer.'

'Sit down, please,' he said. She sat, barely contained. He read her her rights.

'You will speak to your lawyer,' said Philip.

They took her to Mark Robinson, the custody officer.

'Where is my husband?'

They gave instruction for her lawyer to be contacted and left to get Mr Ezogie. He looked very fearful.

'Where is my wife?'

Philip said, 'John Ezogie, we will need to detain you for further questioning. I am arresting you for the abduction of your niece, Grace Edotie.' Philip read him his rights as well.

Ezogie seemed to collapse into himself and Toks was not shocked to see the wetness spreading on the front of his trousers and dripping to the floor. It was not new to her. 'We will need to question you some more once your lawyer arrives.'

Twenty

Toks carefully brushed her hair as she examined herself in her bedroom mirror, feeling a twinge of guilt. She was preparing to go to Coretta's house for dinner. But, should she be? There was a child missing, and a murdered one yet to be identified. An officer had visited the Ezogie's relative in Kent and they were relieved that a child called Ogo was identified as the Ezogie daughter. She had been taken into temporary social care with her siblings. But that didn't mean they could trust the rest of their story. Toks was to call Nigeria tomorrow and check out the address the Ezogies provided for Grace, while Katherine and Roly Poly attempted to find new leads on Venus. Tonight she would have to try to enjoy herself.

The brown Lycra body under her flowery chiffon blouse had given her a deep cleavage. She was glad that the blouse hid that extra roll of fat around her waist. She needed to resume her exercises at the gym. Her mind wandered to the plan for the next day. She and Bode were off to some fancy hotel in Kensington to meet Femi. She had refused for him to come to the house when he suggested it. The hurt and resentment had still not completely disappeared. Tok's mind travelled to Philip and his puzzling behaviour—sticking her with Katherine and telling her he was onto another aspect of the investigation without telling her anything else. She sprayed on one of her favourite scents and, with a last glance at the mirror, picked up her bag and left the room. She was alone tonight. Bode had gone to spend the evening with his friend, Darren. She yawned a little bit as she left the house. She must catch up on some sleep.

***

Coretta laid out her feast in the dining room and looked at the finished work. She loved Waitrose—they were a lifesaver when you needed it. The duck pate, tender lamb slices, steamed vegetables, veggie pastries and different types of cheese all came ready-to-serve. She would bring out the lemon and mango sorbet later. They had invited Paul, one of Richard's friends and a colleague, to make a foursome. She hoped Toks would take to him. She smelt Richard's citrus aftershave before feeling his hands around her waist. She had given him the Armani for his birthday. She rested her head against his chest.

'We haven't done this in a long time,' he said.

'Yes, I guess.' Coretta's voice grew cautious. She had deliberately avoided having long chats with him. She didn't want to tell him that she would be travelling to Nigeria soon. She had read the notebook. Ukeria was a woman of little words and quite expensive. For £1,500 she had written a name and

146

an address somewhere at Bishops Avenue, and a telephone number that belonged to someone in Nigeria. Coretta could not speak to Ukeria because she was sick. Her prison contact told her that she was suffering from a stomach bug. Coretta had used her sources to check information on the address at Bishops Avenue. The property belonged to a Chief Folarin, a billionaire Nigerian businessman and philanthropist who had homes scattered around the world. There was not much else known about him. She would do more research. She also called the phone number in Nigeria and told the person on the other side that Ukeria had sent her. It had been very hard to understand him but finally it seemed he had said, 'Come and see me in Benin.' She had told him quickly that she was speaking from London and he kept saying, 'You come see me. In Benin. Come see me. Someone will text the address to you.' He put the phone down. She had called Margaret who told her that she had to go see the man.

'But, this means I have to go to Benin,' protested Coretta. 'Based on what? What is wrong with speaking on the phone?'

'This is very unsafe for me. Please don't call again. Go and see him and then give him the rest of the money. Don't call here again. My sister is sick because of you. Just go. We have given you what you want. Okay?' And she cut the line. When Coretta had called again there was no answer. It looked as though she was at a dead end and had been ripped off. Then the text came from Ukeria's contact with an address in Benin. She really needed to decide if the trip would be worth it. There was also no contact from Victor who seemed to be ignoring her calls. She had gone to his flat and knocked on the door one rainy day, but no-one answered. The neighbour could tell her nothing.

She would go again tomorrow.

'A penny for them,' said Richard.

'Sorry.' She pulled away from him and tried to put the finishing touches to the table.

'It looks perfect,' he said. 'Let's go away somewhere. Maybe a weekend in Italy.'

'We could go to Nigeria,' she said lightly. And nearly bit her tongue. Taking Richard on her investigation was the wrong idea, her brain screamed.

His face brightened. 'What a good idea. Melissa will be pleased. It's the right time as well as I can finish off my research over there. I have a contact at the University of Lagos who promised he would help me.'

He lifted her up and gave her a deep, lingering kiss. Coretta let herself melt into him. They pulled apart reluctantly when the doorbell rang. Richard watched her with longing as she left the room. Sometimes she hid so far away it was hard to reach her. He put his hand through his hair which sprung back to its unruly state. He hated when she started a new project. She became obsessed and distant. The trip to Nigeria might allow them to relax a little bit. By the time he went to meet their guests he felt light-hearted.

***

The Ezogie investigation was in full swing, but Philip couldn't help stepping out to do his own reconnaissance into Austin. He sat in his car, engine off, staring at a mansion in Farnham, Surrey. It was set in lush acres of land but his information had said that it was a regular haunt for satanic worshipers. An hour passed and the cold began to seep through his skin in icy tendrils, a reminder that he did not belong here. He was grateful a row of wide trees hid his old Mazda 1988, while offering a good view of the winding driveway and the massive gate that barred his access. The place was registered to Turnbull Corporations, which belonged to Mark Turnbull, a wealthy businessman who had made his money during the dotcom boom. It was a conference/entertainment centre and, according to google, was used for weddings. This was no place for a lone walker or car. He could see a dark globed camera on the gate. Since getting there at about eight he had only seen a few people drive out, and they looked like employees. He shivered again and his mind journeyed to Emily. She was definitely going to be rehoused now. He bit his lip and rubbed his hands together. She had changed recently. Instead of the non-stop frenetic movements and the endless chats, she just gazed at him through dull eyes. He didn't know which pained him more, the crazy, shouting Emily, or this one. Philip stiffened as a slow, deep engine cruised by and he saw the flashy behind of a black jaguar with dark tinted windows. The lights came on and the high steel gates slowly opened inwards as the car eased in. Another engine sound. This time a silver Mercedes that came to a standstill when the gate did not open.

A uniformed chauffeur jumped out and talked into what looked like an intercom. The gate opened. Philip felt hope receding as a series of sleek, expensive cars continued to arrive and drive through the gate. He would never catch Austin if he was a part of this set. Maybe he had moved up in the world. Apart from the chauffeur, he had not been able to glimpse a single person. At about ten the cars stopped coming. He had counted just over 20. He mentally checked the other addresses and wracked his brain. Austin, as far as he had known him then, had not been rich. He hadn't despised money, but he also wasn't ostentatious. He liked to control his situation and environment, and was very secretive. This parade wouldn't be his thing. It was too showy. Philip decided to go back and research the addresses again. He must not have done his homework properly. He would search for the smallest and least conspicuous of the locations. That might be Austin. It was a pity that he couldn't track down the man in a conventional way. As far as the system was concerned, Austin didn't exist. He felt the usual seep of despair and guilt. Why was he neglecting a very important case for this? But this was a priority too, he told himself. It was important that Austin did not ruin another woman's life as he had done Emily's. Toks would survive with Katherine. And if his instinct about her was right, Katherine should be the one to watch out.

***

Toks stretched with contentment and grinned at Coretta's

satisfied smile. They had finished their Waitrose meal, for which she had properly scolded her friend.

'Which do you prefer? Us sweating over your jollof rice, or this relaxed way of eating?'

'You cheated!'

They laughed and started loading dirty plates into her hi-tech dishwasher. Every surface in her kitchen gleamed with stainless steel and all sorts of unused gadgets. Paul and Richard were in the lounge. They had offered to do the dishes but Coretta refused and Toks knew she wanted them to catch up on gossip.

'Well, what do you think?' She winked.

'Think?' said Toks, acting stupid.

'Don't play games with me. *Paul!* Do you like him?'

Toks eyed her. 'Is that what it's all about? Poor Toks is lonely, let's find her a partner.'

She saw her friend's stricken look and quickly hugged her. 'I don't mind. He's dishy.'

'Really?' Coretta looked happier.

'You know how I like the intellectual looking types.'

'He's one of Richard's friends at work. He's a writer as well, you know. Published a few books.'

'He told me.' Toks refused to let her know that she had found Paul quite interesting. She liked his intensity. It was a very heady experience.

'So, what have you been up to? We've not had time to catch up,' Toks said, and watched her friend closely. She seemed a little jumpy. Coretta usually updated Toks on her research whenever they met. This time she had said nothing.

'It's okay, I guess. A bit tedious this time.'

'You're not saying much,' Toks pushed.

'Richard and I might be going to Nigeria.'

Toks was surprised. 'Really? Business or pleasure?'

'Pleasure.' Coretta felt bad lying to Toks but it was hard to explain her quest to her friend. She held her breath, not wanting Toks to ask her about the torso case. She did not want to be dissuaded and Toks would be wearing her police hat if she told her.

'You'll be staying with Melissa?'

'Yes. How is your case going?' Coretta changed the subject.

'We have some leads here and there that we're following up. It's just deeply upsetting.'

'Yeah. I'm sure you'll make a breakthrough soon,' she said and stood up. Toks followed suit. She looked thoughtful. Coretta was not telling her something.

***

Toks started to make her calls the next day at the station. She had been given a contact through Interpol and was now trying to get through to a Detective Chief Inspector Tony Ogbe of the CID unit in Benin City. She had sent him an email and was surprised at how quickly he replied. He had left his phone number.

'Hello,' she greeted, once her call was picked up.

'Hello,' greeted a baritone Barry White voice. Toks was

STELLA ONI

intrigued, but quickly squashed the thought. He was probably married with a young mistress tucked on the side. A typical Nigerian man's life.

'Is this DCI Ogbe? It's DC Ade, from East London CID.'

'It is. I hope you are well, Detective.'

'Yes, thank you. I wondered if you were able to check the address that I sent to you? A child called Grace is supposed to be there with her family.'

'DC Ade,' he chuckled. 'We are trying to become more efficient in Nigeria but things still take time. We have contacted the police station in the city nearest to the village and they will be getting back to us today or tomorrow. Hopefully, later today. The village is far from the city but our men are on top of it.'

Toks took a deep breath. 'Thank you very much. Please, if they find the little girl can you email her picture as well?'

'We will try, if we get a picture.'

As the call ended, Toks felt the clock winding down. If things didn't move faster they would be forced to release the Ezogies.

Twenty-One

Toks had still not heard back from Inspector Tony when she left the station and made her way to Kensington with Bode to meet Femi. She glanced at her son's grim face and felt for him. Maybe finally meeting his dad was not such a good idea. She knew it had been eating at him.

'Are you going to share them?' she asked, making her tone casual.

'Uh?' He looked at her, puzzled.

'Your thoughts. Are you nervous?'

'Yep. Not everyday you meet your father for the first time at age 15.'

'Seriously, Bode. Don't be flippant. I know this is hard for you.'

'It is.'

'I'm really sorry.'

'No worries,' he said.

'Well, here we are,' she said lightly as she drove into the premises of the large hotel. 'Are you ready?'

She watched his shoulders lift and her stomach churned.

This was hard.

'Yes,' he said with a sigh. She gently massaged his tensed shoulders and wanted to tell him to let them turn back and go home. They stepped out of the car and she looked at the massive marbled hotel with interest. Her father did say Femi was doing well. A footman in full uniform stood outside the shiny gold entrance.

Toks felt Bode's eyes on her. 'What?' she mouthed.

'You look nice,' he said.

She had put her hair up and wore dark green cord trousers and a matching jacket. The cream blouse beneath strained at her chest, but that could not be helped. The footman bowed smartly and opened the door for them. They walked into a huge reception of ash marble and gold mirrors. Her heels clacked on the shiny floor as they approached a pretty, auburn-haired girl and a sharp young man in a dark suit.

'Can I help you?' asked the girl with a welcoming smile.

'We're here to see Mr Femi Thomas,' she said.

'Ms Ade?'

'Yes.'

'He's waiting for you at the restaurant.' She pointed to the other side of the room at a set of heavy gold embossed doors. The butterflies in Toks stomach went into overdrive. *Why were they called butterflies?* Behind those doors was the man that had broken her heart and fathered her lovely son.

***

Coretta checked her watch as she made her way to Peckham. She was going to sort things out with Victor once and for all. She yawned and smiled as she remembered her night with Richard. He had been ready for them to continue this morning, but she couldn't relax without figuring out what had happened to Victor. They would be having dinner later and could continue where they stopped. She had ignored him for long enough. She looked around at busy Peckham and the rush of people around the shop stalls. The market was supposed to be one of the cheapest around for African food. As she inched nearer to Victor's street, she saw that it got busier and a lot of people seemed to be swarming in its direction. The first thing that came to her mind was to find a way to get out of the place if something was happening. With gun crime rife in the area, it might be best to come back some other time. All the same, she decided to park and walk the rest of the way. Many of the faces seemed tense with excitement and curiosity. As she approached his street, she saw that it was closed off with police crime scene tapes. At a distance, uniformed officers stood watching the curious crowd with impassive faces.

Coretta pushed past a woman carrying a heavy shopping bag. The woman eyed her with dislike.

'What's your problem eh? Did you not see people here who came before you, eh?'

Coretta ignored her and walked on although she started to feel like she was swimming against the current. She found herself no nearer to the police officers but had a better view of the buildings on the street. Officers were at Victor's building!

What was going on? She looked at a man standing to her left. His heavy-jawed face, scoured by three slashes of yoruba tribal marks, was rapt with anticipation.

'What's going on here?' she asked.

'They say a man and a woman have been killed.' Coretta suddenly felt queasy. She tried to calm herself. It could be a coincidence. Things happened in Peckham every day. There were loud sirens as two ambulances drove towards the street. The crowd pressed back and she felt herself pushed against the man she was talking to.

'Do you know who the people are?' she asked.

'No. They said the man was sleeping when they shot him. The woman, maybe his wife, just screamed. The neighbour came out, but she had already jumped.'

The fear gnawed deeper. It was imperative for her to find out who the victims were. She watched as the ambulance crew climbed up the winding stairs but it was hard to know which flat they were going to. She decided to go back to the car to try and call Victor's number once more. For a second, she considered what would happen if it was Victor and the police answered, but they'd have her number from all the calls she'd made anyway. She pushed through the crowd and went back to her car. She listened as it continued to ring. She was about to cut it off when someone picked it up.

'Hello… Victor?' she said. Silence. 'Victor?'

'Hello, is this *Aunty* Coretta?' This was not Victor. This muffled, male voice was deep and definitely one she hadn't heard before.

'Who is this?' she said slowly.

'So… you're Victor's friend eh?' Even as her heart started its rapid, staccato beat, Coretta tried to analyse the voice. It was definitely Nigerian, and it sounded like he was talking with a cloth or something over his mouth. 'Victor can't answer you now. If you call this number again you will be like him. Okay? I have your number. Now we've made sure he can't mess with one of our women.' He hung up.

Coretta's hands shook as she stared at her phone. Her chest heaved as she took ragged breaths and laid her head on the steering wheel. She knew she could not contain it anymore as her voice came out in screaming sobs. She willed herself to calm down but the tears continued to gush down her cheeks. She had not only led a man to his death, but the killer also knew her name and number.

***

As they neared the double doors that would lead them to Femi, Toks stole a glance at Bode and felt sad at how anxious he looked. She thought of how Femi had treated her when she told him she was pregnant. It was hard not to feel bitter towards him. He had told her to get rid of the baby because he had better things planned for his future. At university, everyone had recognised them as a couple so it had been inevitable that people believed they would marry someday. They pushed through the doors and entered the room. He sat alone at a table in the empty, plush room of high ceilings and more gold decorations. He was not looking their way so she had time to quickly study him. He looked well. He had the kind of handsome, sculpted Arabic features that northerners in Nigeria possessed. His mum had been a Fulani from the north who had married a Muslim Yoruba man. She remembered his anger when barely a year after her death his father had remarried. She had comforted him. He looked up and saw them. Their eyes finally met and she was tugged by old feelings. He looked much older of course, but she could still see much of his younger self. He walked from the table and held out his hands.

'Toks… this is unbelievable. Thanks for agreeing to see me.' He held her and kissed her cheeks. She inhaled his smell and felt heat rise to her cheeks. 'And this is Bode? How are you?' He held out his hand. Toks watched father and son formally shake hands.

'I'm fine,' Bode answered, his voice hoarse.

'Let's sit down.' She realised his hands trembled as he pulled the chair out for her to sit and felt bleak satisfaction. He would do all the hard work today. Let him try to catch up on 15 years of their son's life.

***

Coretta felt like she had been sitting in the car for hours. The phone rang again. She held it up with shaking hands. *Anonymous.* She did not know whether to answer it or not.

'Hello?'

'Is this Coretta Davies?' It was a different voice. English.

'Yes?'

'This is Philip Archer at the Peckham major crimes unit. We are making some inquiries about Victor Essam. Do you know him?'

Coretta hesitated. 'Yes, but not very well.'

'May I ask in what capacity?'

'I used to buy African Art from him.'

There was a long pause.

'I'm sorry to say that he's dead. We're calling because we found your number on him and would like to ask you some questions. We're talking to everyone he knows. I would like to request your presence at the station or we can come to talk to you.'

'I'll come.'

She decided to make one more call. It was time she spoke to Toks.

Twenty-Two

Toks watched her son with his father and knew that he was going through some intense emotion. He looked her way as she sipped her drink. She smiled at him then grabbed his hand under the table. His fingers closed over hers and she felt his tension ease a little.

'What are you ordering?' Femi asked him in a gentle voice.

Toks saw those light brown eyes pleading with Bode's identical ones.

For what? She could imagine her boy tipping the table over and walking out of the room. He rarely showed that kind of temper, but he was probably angry with both of them.

'I'm not ready,' he answered. He dropped her hand and stood up abruptly. 'I need to go out for a bit.'

She did not try to stop him as he stumbled out of the room. He wasn't wearing his jacket and, although they had a bit of a sunny break, it was still extremely cold. He would be back soon.

There was silence between them for a while. She snuck a look at Femi and saw his devastated face as he stared at the door, willing Bode back.

'He'll be fine,' she finally said. 'He's just trying to take it all in.'

'He's a fine boy. You've done well, Toks.'

'I don't need your praise, Femi. Keep it.' They stared at each other. 'Why do you want to see him after all this time? I don't want his life de-stabilised. We've done very well so far as you can see.'

'You know you played a part in that,' he said. 'I tried several times... Are you going to tell him that?'

'As far as I'm concerned, you never wanted him. You denied he was your child, remember?'

'Toks...we were 20! And I have regretted it ever since. I was young, ambitious and scared.' He stretched his hand and covered hers. She coolly took her hand away.

'And afterwards? You didn't start asking after him till he was 10. How do you think I felt?'

'I know. I was more comfortable then. I had been so busy. It was hard, Toks.'

'For whom? I was the single parent in Britain.'

'I hope you can both forgive me. Binta died of cancer 2 years ago.'

Toks did not let him know she had heard about his marrying Binta, the daughter of an oil magnate. No wonder he had become wealthy.

'We have a daughter, Aisha. She's 10. She knows she has a brother and is eager to meet him. I'm sorry that I waited till now. Forgive me, please.'

They went quiet as Bode returned. He looked cold. She saw Femi quickly wiping his eyes. Bode avoided looking at them as he sat down.

'I'll order now.' His voice was rough and she felt like crying. What had she let them in for? Maybe she should have left well alone. She shot a nasty look at Femi. He was looking with reddened eyes from her to Bode. What did he imagine? That his son would embrace him with open arms? He had a long way to go.

***

Coretta was glad Richard was not in when she got home. She went straight to her study and laid her head on her desk. The worn down wood cooled and comforted her a little. She had tried to contact Toks but her phone was switched off. Then she remembered Toks and Bode were meeting with Femi today. That alone would be traumatic for them.

Victor was dead. Someone had killed him. And his sister. She ran to the toilet and threw up her grainy breakfast on the white and gold tiled floor before she even reached the bowl. She sat retching till there was nothing more. *She was in way over her head.* Who were these people? She raised herself up from the floor using the bowl for support. The sour smell reeked all over and she began to wipe the floor. Doing the chore cleared her mind and she finally made a decision. The best way to get any information was to go for that appointment with the police. She washed her face and glanced in the mirror. Her face was pale with eyes wild and bloodshot. She hoped Victor's death was nothing to do with the errand. At this moment her only hope was to go on that trip to Nigeria. Coretta was beginning to question her own judgement. What could she achieve there anyway? The Met had sent their men out there and nothing came of it. Maybe she should give up on this and get another project. But no, there were too many loose ends. She checked her time. It was now 5 and Richard wouldn't be back till 7. She'd go to the station. The earlier she got that over with the better. She had a lot of contacts in the force anyway. Maybe she should have started with them first.

Twenty-Three

When she got to the station, Coretta was pleased to see Detective Sergeant Sam Barn, one of her contacts. She didn't like the grim look on his face.

'How are you?' she asked.

'Not bad. What have you got yourself into this time, Coretta?'

She tried to smile. Next to him was another man. A tall detective with a thin face, long Grecian nose, and glinting, intelligent eyes.

'This is DS Martins. We would like to know your connection to this one, Coretta. It's bad.'

'He was an informant,' said Coretta. 'He was supposed to lead me to the people that smuggled his sister into the country. At least, that was the plan.'

DS Martins' phone rang and he left the room. Coretta was happier to speak alone with Sam.

'Well, I think they either got him or he got himself mixed up with something else. Here.' He pushed some photos to her. 'Look at it quickly before Martins comes back.'

Coretta felt the bitterness of bile at the back of her throat. The victims in the crime photo looked unrecognisable. Someone or something had bludgeoned them. They looked swollen and misshapen. Both victims were lined on the floor side by side. She turned her face away and swallowed a dry sob.

'The beating was done after they were dead. They each have a gunshot wound to the head—execution style—and died instantly. This is rage. We'll find them,' he said with assurance. 'We need to know everything you know about this man, Victor Essam. You might be in danger, Coretta.'

So his sister had not jumped to her death? That must have been crowd rumour. She decided it was better to tell Sam as much as was needed. Victor must have found out something important and been killed for it. She bit her lip.

'I'll tell you as much as I know, but in return I'd like to know how you'll resolve this.'

'Coretta, you're in no position to negotiate. Now start speaking.'

***

Toks switched her phone on and glanced at Bode. He looked less angry. Things had lightened up a bit. He was even asking his father questions. She saw how alike they looked with their heads almost close together. For the first time that night she felt that this had been the right decision.

Four missed calls. Coretta and Philip. She tensed as she

listened to the messages. Coretta sounded distressed, but Philip's message sent chills through her. Another clay pot discovered in Ardent Park, Hackney. He had called only about ten minutes before. She checked her watch. It would take her about an hour to get to Clapton, and worst of all she would be deserting Bode when he needed her support the most. They had stopped talking and were looking at her. *So similar.*

'Bode, we have to go,' she said. Femi frowned. 'It's a case I'm working on.'

Bode made to stand up but his father forestalled him. 'I'll bring him later. Would you mind staying longer?' His eyes were fixed on his son. Bode stared back and then finally nodded his agreement. Femi turned back to her.

'I'll drop him off.' His smile was half-pleased and half-pleading. She clenched her fist against her body as resentment filled her. *You've been away for 15 years and already you're taking over.*

She turned back to Bode and looked him deep in the eyes. 'Is that okay with you?'

'Yes, Mum.'

She stood up.

'We'll see you to the car,' said Femi.

'No need.' She gave Bode a brief hug.

'See you soon.'

She turned to Femi. Her eyes held a direct message. *Be careful.*

'I will,' he mouthed.

'See you later, Femi,' she said for her son's benefit.

Twenty-Four

Philip bent and parted the bush to look at the clay pot on the dark mound of earth. This park was one of the smallest in the area, with a few trees and some large bushes. The pot, discovered by a man walking his dog, had been placed by an evergreen bush. The smell of rotting flesh was overpowering and he pressed a handkerchief to his nose. Along with the small pieces of what he now knew as yam and plantain floating in the red palm oil, there were also dark bloated chunks of meat which were unmistakably part of the human body—fingers. He counted 5, along with other parts that Dr Rothman would have to sort out in the lab. Insects, along with a host of maggots, swarmed the pot. The entomologist would have something to work with.

He heard voices coming nearer and looked up. Olive Rothman joined him.

Uniforms had searched the Ezogie's house and packed Grace's remaining belongings for examination. They had not yet found evidence to connect the couple to the crime except for yam and palm oil in the kitchen, which was staple food found in most African homes.

'I think it is the same child,' he said.

Rothman bent over the pot. SOCO had already done their job and the area was secure.

Philip rubbed his eyes. 'It was found by a man walking his dog… he's being treated for shock.'

Katherine joined them and he saw Toks coming in the distance.

'The earlier we can check the DNA for Grace against this, the better,' said Katherine. Toks joined them.

'It looks a good few weeks old, judging by the decay. DNA is being sped up so anytime now, really. In the meantime, I'll try and match these parts,' said Dr Rothman.

***

Toks stared at the clay pot and felt the nausea rising. She had seen worse cases as a uniform, but what if this was little Grace. She looked at the sparse trees and bushes. This excuse for a park was now empty of families who had been innocently playing around this thing. She found it difficult to comprehend how this person operated. Philip watched Dr Rothman prodding in the pot with gloved hands. He came to stand beside her.

'Sorry to call you back. But you can see….'

'Do we have anything else on the Ezogies?' She knew she sounded abrupt.

'We're waiting on the child's DNA. Rothman will let us know very soon, maybe even today.'

'How about Venus?' she asked.

He looked at the pot. 'I'm hoping she's not part of this.'

'This is so evil…' she said.

'That's why it's up to us to stop it.' She saw him looking at her with a rare, gentle look. She was not used to that.

***

Coretta chatted with Melissa about their trip to Lagos. She was now determined to get to the bottom of her investigation. There would be no more crying and lamenting. Victor and his sister must not die in vain.

'We should arrive in Lagos by the weekend,' she said. 'Are you ready for us?'

'Of course. We'll have fun!' said her sister.

'You know I'll need to do that quick spot of travel out of Lagos first,' she warned.

'Where do you want to go? One of the drivers will take you.'

'I have to go to Benin.'

'Benin? What's happening there? Coretta, when will you stop all this business? After all, you have your property portfolio thanks to Richard's family starting you off. Can't you do something else now?'

Coretta scrunched up her face. She hated being reminded of that. Richard's mother never ceased to let her know that it was his grandmother's legacy that had made them so comfortable. Coretta pushed the thought away.

'You'll have to entertain Richard while I'm gone.'

'What?' her sister sounded panicked. 'You know I'm not as clever as Richard. What will I do with him?'

'Joking. He's linking up with some professor at the University of Lagos. You don't need to worry about him. He'll be fine.'

'Right. Mum and Dad said they're not coming yet. I bet you it's Dad. How can he keep staying away from his own country?'

Coretta refused to get drawn in. 'I'll call you later, Melissa.'

'As you wish. I know you're always on his side. Bye.'

Coretta put the phone down and stared at her piece of paper. It sounded like a bit of madness. She was going to Nigeria with only this phone contact as a link, and the name of a Chief whom she had googled. Ukeria was still sick and Margaret had made herself unavailable. The beauty of investigative writing was that everything was an ingredient that could go into the final mix. If the police caught the traffickers then she could still write about that, and Victor and his sister's death would not be in vain. She felt a pang thinking about both of them. She stood up. She was meeting her sister Katie for lunch. She needed to prepare herself. It was always a challenge with her.

***

Toks watched as Chief Superintendent Amos expertly answered the questions thrown at him by the press. With the latest discovery, and the Ezogie's involvement, they were now firmly under the spotlight. The media, always ready to look for scapegoats, had gotten hold of information. She remembered some of the more colourful headlines:

"Savage ritual sacrifice on the increase in London."

"Couple might be connected to savaged child."

Parents were warned to be extra vigilant of their children. Jackson had told the team that a forensic psychologist was now involved in the case. A few of the officers had scoffed at the idea. After all, they had their suspects and proof was the only thing required. Jackson said the idea of the psychologist came directly from above. Toks watched Philip and Katherine. She was sure that there was something between them. She was meeting with Mary Clarke, and knew that she would be entertained by her brash Irish humour, and of course a spot of gossip about him. Maybe it was time she understood how things worked in the department.

After the press meeting, they trooped to the conference room to hear the psychologist. Bode was on an outing with Femi. Apparently, things had gone well with them when she left.

Dr Elsa Townley, a short woman with brown hair and solemn eyes, was already in the room and in whispered conversation with DCI Jackson. Once they were all seated, she introduced herself.

'Thank you for inviting me here.'

An officer snorted in the back of the room.

She continued. 'I want to ask a question. Do you agree

or disagree with me that the killing of this little girl, and the manner in which she was killed, is not all it seems? I want to know what you think.'

Hands shot up immediately. She picked garlicky Blackstone who said, 'I think we got the right people and need to spend our time nailing them.'

A lot of officers nodded vigorously, and Toks agreed. She was not sure they needed Dr Townley at this late stage.

'Another question. Do you believe that the murder of this child was done alone by this couple?' A few people shook their heads. 'So, please explain what you believe.'

Katherine raised her hand. 'They're in custody now, so their accomplices must still be carrying out their work. We just need to link them.'

'Thank you! My job this morning is to be able to point you in the right direction.' She looked around the room.

'What are you trying to say, Dr Townley?' asked DCI Jackson.

'This person does not seem afraid to put their clay pots in well-known public parks. I have to tell you now that the couple you're holding don't fit the profile of this killer, but I believe they know something. You're looking for someone who is methodical and precise in their planning. Which sadly means, there will be more to come.'

'Dr Townley,' said Philip, 'why the ritual?'

She looked thoughtful for a moment then said, 'Fanaticism. It is fanaticism at the heart of it. Perhaps masked as something else but that is my analysis. Check your data again. The answer is there.'

Toks surreptitiously studied everyone around the table. DCI Jackson looked doubtful. Katherine was openly staring at Dr Townley with contempt and Philip's eyes looked dead. She suddenly had an idea and planned to share it with him as soon as they left the room.

Once the meeting was over, she called Philip to the side and told him. She was pleased to see some fire in his eyes. The way he looked the past few days had been worrying.

'That's a good one. Maybe the Dr has a point and we need to follow the heart but in our own way. Go and check for the pots in the African shops in Peckham and maybe Brixton and let's see if that will come up to something. Are the police in Benin still insisting that there is no one at that address in the village?'

She shook her head, conscious of Katherine's laser eyes on them. Maybe they should have gone to Chris's Café.

'They were told that the occupants had gone deep into the hinterland to their farm and normally stay there for days. They also said that they spoke to the neighbours and that two little girls live there. It is not clear if they have always lived there. They promised we will hear something soon.'

Twenty-Five

It had been a long time since Toks visited Peckham and she was amazed at the traffic of people and the number of new shops that had sprung up since she was last there. Her final destination was the long row of shops that sold African food on Rye Lane. She was following a gut feeling. She had parked at the local supermarket and would do some shopping on her return. She walked down the busy road as red double-decker buses whizzed past. She fed her eyes on the shop windows and reminded herself that she needed to get some cash. Toks could already smell the raw meat from the butchers shops. Most were manned by Asian food sellers but a few by Africans. There was a particular shop she was looking for and she almost punched the air when she found it. She entered to the smell of dried fish and earthy live snails. Toks imagined Little Eva's killer buying all of the items in the clay pots from one shop and was filled with fresh purpose.

She approached the woman behind the till. 'Good afternoon, madam,' she greeted.

The woman mumbled, her head bent counting money.

Once satisfied, she looked.

'Good afternoon, ma. Can I help you?'

'Madam, I'm looking for clay pots.' She held out her hands to demonstrate the size.

The woman pointed to a corner in the back.

'We don't sell a lot. There are some there.'

Toks eagerly walked to the back. There they were. Of varying shapes and sizes as well. The ones they'd seen were dark, almost black with patches of brown. These ones were a light brown colour. She was disappointed. What did she think she would find here? And why would she not find it? She argued with herself. The pots were commonplace in Nigeria. The question to ask is why they were here in the UK, and who was using them. She shivered. *Who were these people? Why were they in the UK?* In Nigeria, the government was battling ritual killings. It was commonplace in different parts of the country. Something tingled at the back of her mind. A thread. Could it be something she came across recently? She felt the woman staring at her and got a bag of *gari* and another of pounded yam and took them to her.

'You don't have the dark pots?' she asked.

'No,' the woman looked at her sharply. 'The dark ones are not very common. Only one or two people I know sell them.'

Hope surged through Toks at her words. 'Where are these people?'

'One has a shop in Brixton and the other in Deptford. I say only the people I know, but others might sell them. They bring them from a far, far village in Nigeria.'

'Which village?'

She thought about how they were trying to track down little Grace in Mofa Village. Was there a tie there?

'Somewhere in Benin, I think.' She bagged Tok's shopping and collected the money. 'Try the two people.' The woman gave Toks her change.

'Thank you, Ma,' she said. Toks wrote her number on a piece of paper and gave it to her. 'If you remember the village, please call me. I am a writer and researching the history of clay pots.' The lie came out so well that she nearly ruined it with a smile. She would let Coretta know she had taught her well. The woman looked relieved. *Why was she relieved?* Toks sighed inwardly. Everybody seemed to be a suspect now.

Searching for the two shops she mentioned would have to be a task for another day, she thought as she headed back to the supermarket.

Twenty-Six

Despite what he had promised himself, Philip was back on his hunt for Austin. The brownstone building he was staking out that night was one that he had overlooked for being too small. The little stretch of street was made up of dingy, graffiti-spattered shops which were all shut, leaving the area deserted at 11.30pm. He knew he was somewhere in the South East of London but had lost count of places and directions, having just punched its address into the navigator and followed. He ran his hand wearily over his eyes which felt gritty from sleeplessness and took a long sip of his coffee from a thermos flask. He stared at the building with a small shuttered shop frontage. He had seen lone people walking into it since he arrived a couple of hours back. Some had strolled in casually and others looked furtive. He raised the collar of his jacket and decided he would take a chance and join them. Austin could have slipped past as some of the faces were hidden by hats. He would take no chances. He rubbed his hands to create some heat as the cold wind continued to lance through his jacket. He walked to the building with his head down, following the shape of a woman in front of him. She was wrapped in a large coat and wore a hat, but he could still make out her feminine figure. She stopped at the building and pressed a bell. He heard a voice on the intercom, she muttered something and the door buzzed. She pushed through and Philip sprinted after her. She looked at him, startled, and he had a quick impression of soft brown eyes, smooth skin and arched brows. He nodded solemnly and she nodded back. He must have done the right thing because she inclined her head towards the set of stairs that confronted them and started climbing. At the top, he followed her sound-less steps as his own shoes echoed their approach down the hallway. He regretted not wearing his trainers. Philip knew he was about to witness a black mass if this was a satanic group. He felt the little hairs on the back of his neck spike to attention like brush bristles as they approached a set of closed doors. She held it open for him and he entered before he realised she had disappeared into the gloom. He could not make out much except an impression of a small hall with chanting black hooded figures huddled on the floor. At the other end of the space was a lit altar with a large upside-down cross, a black triangular chalice and some other artefacts. The place reminded him of his boyhood catholic altar except that everything seemed skewed. It was hard to explain but it made him dizzy. As he continued to stare into the gloom he could see nothing more. A few new arrivals darted curious glances his way and Philip decided it was time to leave. Once he got out into the fresh, sharp air he felt better. As he walked to the car he tried to work out his next move. There was no way he could locate Austin in the place. So, now what?

He took a deep breath and his shoulders slumped. He would have to give up on Austin and instead concentrate on helping Emily recover. It was time to move on. As he walked back to the car, a man approaching in the opposite direction stared at him. He didn't care. He entered the car and was about to start the engine when he felt it. The hair on the back of his neck prickled and his scalp tightened with tension as he realised that the atmosphere in the car was different. Then he heard the cold voice.

'Now that you've found me, don't bother looking round. Drive.' Austin pressed something hard against his neck. A knife!

'How did you get in my car?' asked Philip, calmly.

'How do you get in any car? I have my ways, Philip. Now drive and don't move. You understand, don't you?'

Philip started the engine.

***

Toks was in her room, staring at nothing even as the evening news blared out of the TV. She had just given Femi a massive telling off on the phone earlier after the shock of returning home to find Bode's room filled with shopping bags. She had counted about 10! The man had spent £3,000 on their son in one afternoon. *£3,000*. Was he mad? How could he spend that on clothing for a 15-year-old!

'I should have followed you. This is not sensible!'

Bode looked unconcerned.

'No worries, mum. I'm grateful you didn't.' He grinned.

'Bode, I'm not happy about this kind of shopping and I'll be talking to your father.'

'What do you want to say to him? He's trying to make up for not seeing me all these years. And mum? *He's loaded.* I have a rich dad!'

'Bode, you know that you could do a lot more with the money that was spent this afternoon. You could save it towards your driving lessons and a car for when you turn 17. That was the plan and you already have some savings towards that. Why didn't you tell him to just give you the money?'

'No need for that, Mum. He's promised to give me a good allowance and he's buying me the car. We're cool.'

Toks wished she had been more vigilant. Ritual sacrifice or not, this was her son. Femi was going to ruin everything she had painstakingly nurtured in the last 15 years.

'Bode, I felt it was important for you to meet your father. You know that.'

'Don't worry,' he smiled. 'You didn't abandon me. You went to do important work.'

Toks felt she had lost control of the conversation. It was as if he was hiding behind a high wall. What a mess. She shook her head.

'I'm sorry I left you with your father this afternoon. *I'm really sorry.*' Tears sprang to her eyes.

'Mum, I'm fine. I really am.' As he said this, he picked up a pair of trainers and tried them on before showing them off to her with an excited smile. She left the room and called Femi.

'You cannot buy him,' Toks had shouted into the phone. 'If you want to make up with him it's not by buying him, okay? There are other ways you can do it. And Mister, you need my permission in the future. He has not been your son for 15 years and you can't just creep out of the woods and claim that privilege.'

'Shall we try again?' he had begged. 'I have to leave for Lagos tomorrow, but I'm back again in a week or so. How about we start all over?'

'You've already done enough damage. That is not how to get close to him. You should know that.'

His voice was sober as he replied.

'Toks, I'm serious about winning Bode round. He looked really pleased when I dropped him home today.'

'What do you think? If someone bought you all the designer gear you've ever dreamed of in one afternoon *you'd* be happy.'

'I hope he gave you your present,' he said.

'No. And Femi, I don't want a present from you. I just want our son to get to know his father. As you now know, my job takes me away at pretty inconvenient times.'

'I understand. We'll try again when I come back next week. I'll give you a call from Nigeria.'

'What am I supposed to do about what you've already bought for him? I've got a good mind to tell him to return them.'

'Toks. Leave him. It was my mistake. Let him enjoy this

and we'll start over when I come back.'

She said nothing.

'Toks?'

'Yes?'

'I've really missed you. You haven't changed much. You're still so beautiful.'

She allowed a long pause while she gathered her thoughts. This man needed to be made to understand some things.

'Femi. If you want to have a relationship with your son, make sure you leave me out. We will repair this afternoon's damage and that is all.'

'I'll see you in a week,' he said gently.

Now Toks turned to look at the gift – a brown Mulberry handbag that was soft and pliant to the touch. A picture of how it would match some of her outfits came unbidden and she ruthlessly squashed it. She would give it back to Femi when he returned. She got into bed and laid her head on the pillow, knowing it might be awhile before she slept.

Twenty-Seven

Philip had been driving for about fifteen minutes with the knife still pressed against his neck. The pressure exerted by Austin was drawing blood. He could feel the warmth trickling down. He knew he was being directed to some isolated area and was proven right when Austin commanded him to stop off a little road opposite a big cemetery.

'Turn too quickly and I'll hit your jugular,' he warned.

Philip's head throbbed.

'Now answer this. Why were you following me?'

Philip found it difficult to speak as sweat beads formed like icicles on his forehead.

'I ask again. What did you want?'

'What did you... do... to Emily?' He finally forced the words out.

'I did nothing to her.'

'You did something. Why did you... visit?'

Philip found what happened next hard to explain later. He attributed his memory loss to the pain caused by the pressure of the knife. One-minute Austin was behind him and the next he was on the passenger seat and had pulled his head so close that Philip felt pierced by the ice in his eyes.

'I did nothing to your sister. Just let her end her days slobbering and gibbering. She made a pact and she's paying what she owes. Don't think of following me again, Philip. Accept your sister for what she is. You're in over your head. This isn't your fight.'

His voice drilled into Philip's head and he felt his ears starting to pop and strain with the pressure. He tried to hold his head and realised his arms felt leaden and he could not lift them up. He could feel blood streaming down his nose and a burning pain on his arm.

'Your knife is poi…snd,' he said, but his tongue felt thick and clumsy.

Austin laughed. 'Thanks to the Incas. They have blessed us with many potions. This one will teach you a lesson.'

With a silent scream, Philip slid into darkness.

The burning pain on his arm and neck woke him up. He winced as he raised his head from the steering wheel and eased himself back on the seat. Then it all came rushing back and he whipped his head round to look at the back seat, but knew it was empty. Austin had escaped. He touched the back of his neck and felt the line of crusted blood. He knew he would look a mess if he saw himself in the mirror. He pulled back his sleeve and groaned when he saw the source of the pain. The area near his elbow was covered with a red scab as if he had been burned. *How had Austin done this?* He closed his eyes and cursed under his breath. The time on the dashboard read

1 AM. He had been out a while! He stretched his arm out and checked the mark again. Hopefully with time it would fade. Austin had as much as admitted that he had something to do with what was wrong with Emily. But what did that mean? He shook his head. Satanists, witches—what else? He needed to get out of this place. He would be able to think more clearly when he got home. He made to start the engine and his phone rang.

Rothman.

'Where have you been? I've been ringing you all night!'

'I've been busy,' he replied brusquely.

'I checked the Ezogies' DNA—it's Grace. I've been burning the midnight oil to confirm it.'

He straightened. 'At least we have them.'

He cut the call. His headache was blinding and he groaned again. Loud beeps on the phone made him realise he had messages. 10 missed calls. He listened.

Twenty-Eight

Toks was at the station although she was desperate to go to church. Bode was on drumming duty and had gone by himself. They had too many new developments in the investigation to ignore. She would try to make the evening service. Just then Philip entered with a face so drained of colour it almost matched his stained white shirt. He looked like he had been in a fight with vampires and lost. She waved to him and left for her meeting with Katherine to interrogate the Ezogies. Mrs Ezogie was brought into the interview room. Toks saw that the time in jail had changed the woman. She was a far cry from the confident woman in the first interview. Her curly hair was uncombed and she looked oddly naked without her makeup and jewelleries.

The solicitor was a pink-faced city boy in a grey suit. *Where had they found him? And who was paying his bill?* She promised herself she'd do some digging there.

'My client cannot give you more information than she's already given and there is really no need for this interview.' His drawling voice, a contrast to his looks, immediately wound Toks up. 'After-all, you've found nothing in their possession to link them with the murder of little Grace. They have told you what they know. They trusted the woman to whom they gave the child and they've aided your investigation by giving you her address.'

'They gave us insufficient information,' said Katherine. 'What documentary evidence proves that Grace was entrusted to this woman? We have nothing to show how she came into this country. Your clients have smuggled a child into the country, and that child was abused and murdered.'

Mrs Ezogie seemed to jerk up at Katherine's words and made to stand up to talk, her eyes brimming with tears, but the solicitor forestalled her by raising his hand. She shook her head and glared at him.

'Yes, we made a mistake by bringing Grace in this way but we trusted Deborah to take her home for us. We did!'

'Can you tell us something?' asked Toks, looking straight into the woman's eyes. 'If you took the trouble to use illegal means to bring this child into the country, why then send her back? How do you explain that?'

She kept silent.

'You're likely to go down for this murder. Is her name even Grace? All we have to go on is what you've told us. Tell us exactly what you did and how she died,' said Katherine.

Mrs Ezogie started to shout. 'We were trying to help… we sent her back home with Deborah. She promised she would take her back for us.'

'She was killed and Deborah, the woman you said you entrusted her with, is not at the address you gave us. In fact, they have never heard of her.'

'She has run away. She did something to Grace,' cried the woman.

'Interview terminated,' said Katherine above Mrs Ezogie's loud sobs.

They escorted her out of the room with the solicitor following.

'They know what happened to that girl. I can tell you that now,' said Katherine.

Toks agreed. 'They'll break soon.'

***

Later, she, Philip and Katherine went for their meeting at DCI Jackson's office.

He looked thoughtful. 'So, the Uncle and Aunt are not admitting to abusing and killing the little girl? How about the missing daughter?'

'Grace lived with them,' said Philip. 'There's a lot of evidence from neighbours and we found some of her belongings in the house. The children confirmed she was their cousin and seemed upset that they had stopped seeing her, but the missing daughter, Ogo, was found with an Aunt.'

Jackson pursed his lips. 'Can we tie Grace's killing to them? We don't have a shred of evidence. They've admitted to smuggling her here and insisted they paid for her to be smuggled out. Sounds off. They either did the killing or know about it. We need more.'

'We can't find Deborah, the lady that was supposed to have taken the child out of the country,' said Katherine.

'Can we tie them to all these ritual sacrifices? They must have accomplices. The force has taken too many batterings in the past involving the neglect or killing of children. Damilola, Climbie. We need to put a proper closure on this one, and the earlier the better.'

He looked weary as he picked up his phone. They left and walked into the chaos in the squad room. PC Walton, an energetic and eager young man, had been on his way to them.

'We've got another one. A park near Walworth Road, south London.'

Toks rushed after Philip. They already knew there was a pattern of the killers using parks, but there were too many London parks! They could not police all of them. The public were on the alert, but that had given them more work as they had received a lot of false sightings. She thought about her promise to meet Coretta later that evening.

***

Coretta checked her watch. It was quarter to eight. Toks was supposed to come at seven. She still nursed hope of her and their friend Paul getting together and had persuaded him to come. She felt a bit guilty about putting pressure on Toks in the middle of her investigation. When the doorbell rang at eight she breathed a sigh of relief. She opened the front door to see her friend in a pair of jeans and a t-shirt, holding up a bottle of wine.

'Sorry?' she said with a forced smile, handing the bottle to Coretta who stared at the dark circles round Tok's eyes.

'I'm so sorry I dragged you out. You could have cancelled,' she said, her earlier guilt returning.

'Well, you're away to Nigeria soon and I guess I might not see you before you go.'

'Still, I told Paul he should wait and not go yet,' Coretta whispered as she stole glances at the lounge area where Toks could hear deep voices in conversation.

Tok's eyes widened. 'Paul is here?'

'He insisted. He wanted to see you again.'

'Girl, I'm not in the mood for matchmaking. I can't even eat for what I saw this evening.'

They walked to the kitchen. Coretta put the bottle on the table and turned to her friend. 'Is it the same case?'

'Yes. Today we found her head. Now we can visually identify our girl.' Coretta saw the tears in her friend's eyes.

'Coretta, I've been in the force for over 10 years and I still don't understand it. As a staunch church goer and a believer in the goodness and grace of God we constantly talk about good and evil. But not at this level.'

Coretta kneaded her friend's rigid shoulders. They felt as hard as plank. In the years she'd known Toks she had never seen her this way. She decided to make her own confession.

'Toks? I need to tell you about my trip to Nigeria.' She knew she had her attention. 'I have a contact that promised to tell me more about the boy that was killed and found in the

Thames years ago.'

She watched Toks' eyes widen. 'That was a long time ago! You intend to go?'

'I have too many loose ends in my research. The good thing about writing is if you don't find closure you can still write about the process.'

'But it's dangerous, Coretta. I don't like it! We're liaising with the police in Nigeria and you could be obstructing justice by not passing on information. If it's the same kind of people that killed this girl, then they're ready to do anything to protect themselves.'

Nothing would stop Coretta and she knew that Toks could see that.

'You'll still go?' her friend said with resignation. 'Be very careful. This is not child's play. And the moment you learn anything, you need to tell the police.'

'I'll be careful,' Coretta said. 'Why don't we join Richard and Paul?'

'You think Paul will be enamoured by a red-eyed wreck like me? I must go home, Coretta. I'm in no state to socialise. Please extend my apologies to both of them.'

'Try and get a good night's sleep.' She escorted her friend to the door and watched her drive off. Toks was probably upset with her, but their jobs were different. Coretta could not imagine herself as a police officer. It was too restrictive! She had also not been able to tell her about Victor and her own brush with death. She would wait a few days and then call her. She went to join the men. *So much for matchmaking.*

Twenty-Nine

Philip felt the burning pain on his arm as he stood watching Rothman. The mark looked red and raw as he dressed for work this morning. If only he could remember how the bastard had done it to him. He winced as he brushed his elbow against one of the morgue tables. Olive observed him.

'Are you ok?'

He avoided her gaze. He did not want her sympathy. He had met his former wife, Helen, through Rothman.

'It's nothing. I'm fine.'

'How's Emily?'

'She's up and down most days.'

'You can always talk to me,' she said. Philip did not respond.

Her face became closed and she was all business again. She was working on the latest remains. He watched the pot on the table intently. Rothman's assistant, Siobhan, was efficiently preparing all the instruments by the side of the table. He remembered how officers had gone out in numbers to throw up on seeing its content. Toks had succumbed this time and he had not blamed her. The pot was the same dark clay colour as the others, but larger. It had been filled to the brim with objects. The head, which had been placed on top of everything, was small, dark and bloody. The child's eyes closed, mouth open showing tiny teeth. If she had ever had hair then it had been completely shaved off. He could see nicks on the scalp, possibly where the blade had cut the skin. It was a sight to twist any insides. He felt himself gag and turned away.

'This was also done post-mortem. There's not much blood formed here,' she pointed to the area of the neck. 'From all I've seen so far, I would stick to my first theory that she was drained of blood, or killed and drained, before cutting up her body parts.' She put the head down and started looking at the other contents. She fished them out one at a time. 'Yam, palm oil, cowrie shells. Lots of them in this pot. You'll need to understand the meaning of all this.'

'Yes.' They would have to go back to Professor White.

'Hmmm.' She had brought out everything in the pot. 'The cowrie shells are not the only thing that set this apart. This is a bigger pot. I would have said this was the main sacrifice.'

He watched as Siobhan handed her a saw. She was going to start cutting into the little skull. He knew it was time for him to leave.

'We might have more info by tomorrow?' he asked.

She looked up, saw in hand, her face tight with concentration and possibly fatigue.

'Once we've analysed all of this, yes. You know there is one more to come. Don't you?'

'The torso.'

'Yes, the torso,' she said, and put on her goggles.

***

Coretta watched as Sam Barn drank his cognac. He had a sense of expectancy about him and she knew it was because the afternoon would cost her. He always required 'compensation' and she readily gave it to him. The information he had supplied her over the years had backed up some of her writing. She dared not let Toks know that she had police contacts in her pay.

'What I'm about to tell you will practically write your book, Coretta.'

She suppressed her excitement. 'You made progress on Victor's case?'

'More than that. Do you remember the news about the smugglers that were rounded up in a police raid two days ago?'

Coretta frowned. She hadn't done much relaxing in the last two days. Instead she had locked herself in her study and written the outline of her book.

Sam eyed her with amusement. 'Don't tell me you're slipping! You were always on the ball with every kind of news.'

'Please, update me,' she said.

'We tracked the bastards and, based on information obtained by yours truly, we did a warehouse raid.' He punched his large palm. Coretta knew that Sam was going to charge a lot for this enthusiastic rendition. He liked the good things of life. The expensive glass of drink he had ordered on her bill was evident. His splotchy, red cheeks showed that he might be doing a bit too much of it. 'We arrested eight smugglers and fifteen women living in that warehouse and other houses scattered around London.' His voice was smug with satisfaction.

Coretta sat up straight. 'How did you catch Victor and his sister's killers? How did you know about this warehouse?'

He lifted his hands palms outwards. 'Hey! One question at a time. We found some things in Victor's house that led us to a house in Brixton.'

'What things?' Coretta was starting to get impatient. He always had to milk the situation.

He drew nearer to her. He was bald at the front but still insisted on combing the remaining wisps over his large, pink patch.

'Victor had some nude pictures of a woman—someone called Helena. Very pretty and well-endowed.' She watched his shining eyes and imagined some of his male colleagues secretly poring over the pictures.

'We're still trying to piece it all together. Some neighbours recognised him visiting Helena.' He looked at her slyly.

She waited for him to continue his story. Sam would take his time and watch for the impact of every one of his words. She decided to keep her expression bland. That would teach him. She noticed his disappointment as she curbed her eagerness. That made him talk faster.

'This Helena is a prostitute. Smuggled into the UK under a false identity two years ago. She lived in that house and had made the syndicate a lot of money. Extremely popular and experienced. Victor must have found the place as soon as he started his errand for you. We believe that his sister might have been held at a similar house. Post mortem revealed that she did have a baby as recent as six months ago. You said she told you she had a boy. We're still trying to track him down. Hoping they haven't flushed the poor ticker down the toilet somewhere. We need to get the woman that attended to the birth. Apparently, they are regularly visited by a doctor and a nurse who obviously worked under false names. Anyway, Victor became obsessed with this Helena and would visit her every evening. The smuggler allocated to Helena started getting angry with him because although Victor still paid to have Helena, he was spending too long with her and affecting his other clients. He also took to hanging outside the house and picking fights with any man that came to visit. The syndicate didn't like it. It was causing negative attention. They had stayed quiet so far, with no neighbours bothering to question their comings and goings and one or two enjoying the delights on their street. With Victor and his antics they knew they were attracting attention, so they ordered his killing.'

Coretta felt bad. Indirectly she had caused Victor's death. He had met Helena through the errand he was running for her. But she still puzzled over something. She realised Sam had kept quiet and was watching her. She kept her face still.

'If an execution was ordered, how come Victor and his sister sustained such injuries? They were both shot and then beaten,' she said.

His twinkling eyes told her that he still had her hooked and would reel her in.

'That's Helena's work. They had no idea she was also nursing feelings for Victor. She heard that he was living with a woman and jumped to the conclusion that he lived with a lover. She heard them planning his death and begged the man that was to do the killings—one of her clients, it happens—to take her along with him. We don't know why, but he did. She was high on drugs and fully participated. We were able to link fibres and prints directly to her. After the killer shot them, she kicked the dead bodies till she ran out of strength.'

Coretta could not hide her shock.

'Why?'

'Victor hadn't told her that his sister lived with him.'

Coretta imagined that maybe, even with all his infatuation, Victor had not completely trusted Helena.

'Helena is under arrest, along with all the smugglers and the other girls. We're trying to sort out what to do with them. Some claim to have been forced into this, but they're all illegal and I'm afraid a few are hooked on drugs.'

Coretta moved closer. 'I want as much material as you can supply. Some of my work led you to this.'

The twinkle disappeared and he eyed her coldly. 'You need to be careful. You've stepped on a lot of toes in the department. Do you know that? All those award-winning books and some of those investigations slagging off the force. A lot of people don't like that—you need to start watching your back.'

Coretta studied him and said nothing. She knew where

this was leading. 'I'm putting my job on the line by continuing to give you this info. Questions are starting to be asked about your source. Fortunately, the force understands that writers are very canny and will get info wherever possible. It's going to cost you a lot more this time.'

As the source of most of her police info, he was invaluable. She would pay him what he wanted. 'That's fine. I need your help somewhere else. You know the Alpha case?'

'Who wouldn't remember? We're going through worse than that with the Park rituals.'

'They're connected,' said Coretta.

'How would you know? Child is smuggled into the country. Child is killed and chopped up.'

'I think they're related. Call it a hunch.'

'Well, what do you need?'

'I want information about the group that went to Nigeria. Where they went and how they carried out the investigation.'

He exhaled. 'I'll try and let you know.'

'I need it very soon, by tomorrow.'

'Tomorrow? I thought you'd have enough to write about with what I've given you.'

'I need it.'

'It'll cost you.'

'So be it.'

'Like I said before. Be careful. If you put the force in a good light, you'll have our goodwill. But continue this way and a lot of things could start to go wrong.'

Coretta's eyes narrowed. 'Do I detect a threat?'

'More like a friendly warning. I don't speak for myself. Just watch what you write.' He stood up. 'Let me get to work and get that info for you. Enjoy the rest of your day.'

He left. She sat there for a while deep in thought. She would have to find a way to help to arrange for the burial of Victor and his sister, or else they would end up in a pauper's grave.

Thirty

Toks felt the energy of Brixton as she arrived at the outdoor market. The place always fascinated her. She loved trailing down the long row of stalls on Electric Avenue and observing multicultural Britain at its finest.

Years ago when she did a stint of work here, she would go into the market and buy fresh meat, fish and vegetables for her large winter soups. She still made her soups and recently shared some with Garlicky Blackstone who boasted that he was not afraid of any kind of chilli. She had promised him some hot fish pepper soup once they finished wading through this case. She knew there was no time to stop and browse for food as she headed for the beginning row of shops in the indoor market. The 4th shop was an African one and she went straight for it. The shopkeeper, a woman in black wool trousers and bright red sweater was outside arranging plump tomatoes into plastic bowls. Toks smiled inwardly. You could never mistake the bulging bottom of an African woman.

'Good morning, ma.' The woman looked up with a smile. Toks smiled back. So unlike her reception at the shop in

Peckham.

'Good morning,' she greeted.

Toks eyed the display of abundant baskets of ripe and green plantains, spinach and greens, large and small chilli peppers and decided to enter the shop. The woman followed her in.

She scanned the interior and noted the usual bags of rice, *gari* powder made of dried cassava, and *elubo* powder made from dessicated yam.

'What can I help you with this morning, ma?' asked the woman as she saw the way Toks looked around.

'I'm looking for dark clay pots, small and large.' She curved her hands to indicate the sizes. 'The ones you have here are brown.'

'Oh, I don't have that kind. Very hard to find. These ones are very good as well.' She pointed to some medium sized brown pots on the top shelves.

Toks knew she was now obliged to buy something from her if she wanted more information. 'Anyway,' she said to the woman. 'Let me buy some peppers and okra.' She went out to pick some fresh red peppers and okra and then paid.

The woman looked happier. 'Go down a little bit from here. You will find another shop like this one. The man there has a few pots like the one you're asking for.'

She counted out some change and Toks thanked her. As she walked along, she stopped briefly to look at the display of glistening 'fresh' fish at the fishmonger's. The smell was strong but she had never minded that. Fish was only fresh to her if caught from the sea on the day. Back in those days in Nigeria, her father used to make the special journey to the seaside every Friday evening to buy freshly caught fish. As she walked on, she realised she had lost her concentration and just gone past another African shop. She retraced her steps and looked in briefly. No pots. She walked on and then saw one that was on a larger scale to the woman's, with twice as much stock. The proprietor was a short, squat man in his fifties. He looked Nigerian, possibly from the eastern side but she could not be sure.

'Good morning,' she greeted.

'Morning, Aunty,' he answered with a bright smile.

'I'm looking for small dark pots.'

'Oh, I have a few of them. They go quickly and it takes a long time for me to have new ones. You have come at the right time.' He walked into the shop.

'Here, Ma.' The man brought out several pots.

Tok's heart quickened but she kept her expression neutral.

'I will take one.' She pointed to the exact type that had filled her nightmare for the past few weeks. These were identical to the park pots. 'Do you know anybody else that sells them here?' The man shook his head. 'They're very scarce.' He moved nearer to her, his eyes knowing. 'People have many uses for them, Aunty.'

Her thoughts started racing with possibilities as she studied him.

I could take you in for just saying that. Did he know of the killings? Had she stumbled onto something?

'Would you remember if anyone came to buy plenty of them from you? Maybe more than four?'

The man's eyes narrowed with suspicion. 'Why, Ma?'

'I will tell you something, uncle.' Toks felt the lies tripping off her tongue as quickly as she formulated them. 'I think my husband must have come to your shop. He is trying to *get* me and I know he might buy plenty from you. I too must take care of myself. You know what I *mean*, uncle.'

'I understand, sister. All these people shout, God! God! We know that if we want to get results we must use our own African measures. God takes too long sometimes.'

'Sometimes it's best to wait for Him, then,' Toks said, unable to help herself. He gave her an odd look.

'Since you ask. One woman came to buy plenty of these pots some months ago. I too wondered what kind of big *juju* she was doing that she needed so many, but then sometimes these people like to use our pots for decoration.'

'Which people?' Her voice came out too sharp and she modified it by giving him a small smile.

'These white people. The woman and the man that bought it were white.'

***

Philip sat opposite Professor White and watched him examine each crime scene photograph. He had convinced himself to go. It seemed everyone was busy and he needed some quick expert advice on the latest pictures. Katherine was following some lead and Toks was after the clay pots.

'Hmmm,' mumbled the professor.

He checked each picture over and over again before taking sharp rapid notes, his hairy fingers swift as a spider. Philip felt like scratching the bruise on his arm, still red but no longer hurting. Every time he thought of Austin, he felt shame and anger. 'This is not very good,' snapped the professor, yanking Philip back to the present. 'Pure Nigerian and yet... I don't know... it doesn't seem quite right. Somebody is trying to cover the four corners of London.' He looked up. 'I'm looking at the parks. One in East, South, North. You would know this. Maybe something in the West soon.' He peered at Philip, his eyes unnaturally large behind his lenses. 'I am told you have some suspects in custody?'

'Possibly.'

'Hmmm.' His hand swept over the photographs. 'Each delivery would require elaborate rituals and not just by one person.'

'We are patrolling as many of the parks as possible.'

He watched as the professor smiled, or what passed for a smile. Philip was starting to wonder what he was doing there.

'Do you believe in the supernatural at all, Detective Dean?'

'I don't.'

He watched as the other man licked his lips in anticipation of what he was about to impart.

'In my work I have travelled to various parts of Africa, South America, Caribbean, Southern Africa... places like Nigeria, the former Congo, Brazil, and Haiti. I have learned to respect a lot of the traditions. These people hold deep beliefs.' He waved his hand. 'Though a majority have accepted Christianity, most still go back to the native doctor if the need arises.' His enlarged eyes bore deep into Philip's. 'When a belief is held that deeply then it can be given life by the believer. There's a lot that science cannot explain yet. I have seen things to which I cannot ascribe a rational explanation. Your killers are very keen to make all their sacrifices and that might be their downfall. This must be an appeasing sacrifice. They will have to complete it. We've got the hands, the feet, the head and parts of this poor child's body, but we do not have the torso. If they don't offer the torso, then in their view all may be in vain. This is your chance to catch them.'

'What is an appeasing sacrifice?'

The professor leant forward. 'When they join their cults, they have to promise to sacrifice an innocent to appease the god or deity of the cult.'

'And is it to this god called *Eshu*? Is this like Satanism?'

Professor White shook his head. 'No. *Eshu* in some of their myths is seen as a messenger to gods, especially by the Yoruba tribes in Nigeria. Others see him as an evil trickster and use him to put hexes on their enemies. This sacrifice is used as a big appeasing sacrifice to this god but its function is twisted. I need to give it some thought.'

'Anything more?' asked Philip.

'Have you tried investigating religious groups?' asked the professor.

'Groups? Do you mean like Satanists?'

'This is not the work of Satanists. This is not the way they hold their mass or carry out their ritual. Those ones would have made an even bigger statement by placing these pots in churches or desecrating holy places.' He shook his head. 'No.'

'Have you got any kind of group in mind, professor?'

The man looked reflective. 'You strike me as a man of few words, detective. You will have to be patient with me. There are religious groups even in England like Yemoja, Etueje, Imole, Olokun. Some are highly secretive and might not even register on your systems. But some that call themselves societies or community groups are registered.'

'We know such groups exist and some of our undercover officers have attended meetings. They seem harmless.'

Professor White smiled.

'I suggest you go back and check them again. I believe that a cult did this. It probably involves a lot of money. It could be money that they want undiscovered here.' This reminded Philip of what Dr Townley said to them. Could they be looking at things the wrong way round? He would get the analysts to check this for them.

'Thank you, Professor,'

'I really wish the police luck on this one,' he said. Philip thanked him and left.

Thirty-One

Toks went back to the dark clay pots shop in Brixton. She watched the shopkeeper busily darting from till to customers. When she saw a small lull, she went up to him. She had made up her mind to tell him she was with the police. His eyes widened as she told him that he was now part of her investigation. She wrote her number on a card and gave it to him, disappointed that she could not get any more information about the buyers. Of course, they might have an innocent use for them.

'Please let me know if anyone comes to buy more. Just take their details.'

He stared at the card before putting it in his pocket.

'Madam, I need to ask an important question, now that you have said you are police.'

'Yes?'

'I hope this will not affect my business. I'm not foolish. All the things in the paper recently about the little girl. These my pots – our African people use them for all sorts of things.'

'Nothing will affect your business. You'll have our gratitude, though. I just want to know if anyone else is buying more of your pots.'

And that was that.

She called Philip and updated him. 'I hope he calls me back. I think we might be getting close,' she said. She listened as he told her of his conversation with the professor. She became thoughtful.

'Are you still there, Toks?'

'Yes,' she said. 'I think that Professor might have a point. Maybe things are simpler than we think. I'm on my way.'

Philip was talking to Katherine when she arrived at the station. She joined them.

'I've just come from Jackson,' Katherine said. 'He wants to see us. He's not happy.'

They trooped to DCI Jackson's office. He looked angry. 'DSupt Amos wants to bring in the murder squad to take over. They're going to hijack our case.'

'Did you explain that we have the Ezogies and have charged them with child trafficking? We need more time to gather evidence to charge them with murder,' said Philip.

'They know that. It doesn't look good for us.'

'We know the Ezogies are heavily involved in this,' Philip said.

Jackson slapped the table. 'No bloody help, Philip. We have three days or it's off our hands. So, what do you say, guys?'

'We'll try our best,' said Philip.

'Well, *try*. Don't let those shits tell us how it's done. We're good at this. *Three days.*'

Thirty-Two

The aeroplane landed on the runway with a thud—a sound that made Coretta happy that they had finally arrived in Nigeria. She had warned Richard that Melissa would probably drag them to a function later that night. She needed to ask her sister who this Chief Folarin on Ukeria's note was, and see if anything could come of that. She had not been able to find out much in the UK. The house on Bishops Avenue was empty for most of the year.

She turned to her husband. 'Are you okay?' He had been on his laptop throughout the flight while she enjoyed two movies.

'Yes, I just emailed Professor Emeka to say I'll be seeing him tomorrow.'

'I hope you can. Melissa has a way of hijacking our trips to Nigeria. She'll want to show you around.'

'Not till I get this research out of the way. I can't think why we never came here together before.'

Coretta gave a cynical smile. 'Wait till you see what she's planned for us.'

The plane had stopped. Richard gave her a boyish grin and she regretted that they had not made the trip before. Perhaps Melissa was right. Maybe if their father felt more strongly about his country they would have visited more. She remembered when she told him she was travelling, he had looked so concerned that she had felt some of Melissa's impatience. *It was his country.*

'Be careful, darling girl. I need you to be careful there,' he had said. Even her mother had visited a few times. Coretta had studied his tall, stooped frame and wondered when he had turned into this quintessential British man with all the mannerisms. She would ask him that question one day.

Richard nudged her. The passengers were moving. They would be out of the plane in a few minutes and Melissa had promised the driver would be waiting for them on the tarmac. Her sister never took chances. She would also ensure that their luggage was cleared by customs. They stepped out and she saw Richard sniffing the air. His skin began to glisten with sweat. He looked at her inquiringly.

'What's that smell?'

She grinned. 'Welcome to Lagos. Probably the unique smell of this town or that of the sewers nearby. Who knows?'

They came down the steps with the other passengers. She observed them. There were Nigerians, English 'expats', Lebanese, and quite a few Chinese nationals. She had not networked on this flight. She remembered one transatlantic flight where she had closed a lucrative publishing deal. Melissa's new driver, a slight balding man with sun darkened skin, was waiting for them with a raised placard. Her sister tended to frequently change her drivers.

'Hello, I'm Coretta.'

'Good aftanoon, Madam. My madam said I should collect you and sir.'

They followed him to a sleek black Mercedes. Behind it was a dark Peugeot full of armed men in uniform. This was how Melissa travelled. She always had one or two of these escorts wherever she went. Richard did not seem to be able to take his eyes off them.

'Are *those* following us?'

'At a discreet distance.' She kissed his sweaty, bemused face. 'It's safer because of kidnappers and armed robbers.'

The driver cruised to a line of uniformed men standing near the plane.

'Madam, sir,' said the driver, 'I will need your passports for these immigration people. Don't worry, I will take care of everything.' A phone rang in the car and he picked it up. 'Yes, ma. I have them here now, ma.' He gave the phone to Coretta. 'It is Madam. She wants to speak to you.'

'Hey girl! Happy to know you're here. How was the flight?' cried Melissa.

'Fine, just looking forward to seeing you.' Coretta glanced at Richard. 'Richard is still shell-shocked, but he's feeding his eyes.'

'Tell him I have a lot planned for him.'

'I will.'

'Welcome home. We're going to have some fun.'

'Don't forget that I have some work to do first.'

'You're a workaholic. Relax, enjoy yourself a little bit. You know this place beats England any time.'

'I'll say you said so,' replied Coretta. She watched as the driver approached immigration.

They took the passports from him and stamped them. He came back into the car and gave them back the documents, then they drove off with the dark Peugeot following closely.

***

Toks and Philip were at Chris's café for a break and drink. She was trying to be good and had eaten her homemade salad earlier. But the menu made her mouth water. She refused to bend. The spare tyres and big bum needed to go!

Philip's eyes crinkled in amusement. It suited him. She wished he smiled more. *Crinkle.* That was usually reserved for old Hollywood stars like Mel Gibson or Paul Newman. But they did crinkle. She was impressed.

'Are you sure you don't want to eat anything?' he asked.

'Yes, I am,' she said, sounding prim. 'I will have a large latte though.'

'Right.'

The waitress came to take their order and left.

'I guess we're nearly out of time,' she said.

'Yes,' he said. 'I wanted to say that you've done really well. We threw you in at the deep end and you swam. You should have made the move to detective earlier.'

Toks was pleased. 'Thank you for giving me a chance.'

'You came with great recommendation. I suppose after this, everything might become an anti-climax. It's not all the time that we get major cases like this. It's pretty mundane usually.'

She nodded. 'I understand.'

'I think if you progress like this, you could make Sergeant in a short time.'

'Thank you,' she said. Toks was proud of the confidence he had in her. She looked forward to that meeting with Mary Clarke. She was curious why he was still a DS. It just didn't make sense, his responsibilities were almost that of a Detective Inspector. She could see that Jackson and Amos trusted him.

***

Philip dashed down to visit Emily at her new residential home. Her move had been swift and he had not been around to help. He looked around the lobby. It was well furnished, without clutter.

His mind went back to work. He had given a list of the societies suggested by Professor White to Toks to follow up. The Ezogies had begun to talk at last. Their solicitor was not pleased, but the husband, worn down by the same terror that had plagued him every time they questioned him, told them that he and his wife had lied about the name of the lady that took little Grace from them. He had given them the real name, Margaret Imafidon, and they were now trying to track the woman down and bring her in for questioning. It had been difficult to manage Emily's move and still concentrate on the case. He had caught some puzzlement from Toks and knew that he would have seemed distracted. Most especially as the manager had spent a considerable amount of time trying to understand Emily's history from him. That had frustrated him. Emily had had more social workers than changes of underwear and although over the years a large amount of history had been written down, he still got asked the same questions. He felt that they were all probably too lazy to go back and read their crabby notes.

He arrived at Emily's room, large and cheerful with a single bed, lamp, sink and wardrobe. He was surprised when he found a woman sitting by his sister's bedside talking to her. When she saw him, she stood up and held out her hand. She was African Caribbean, of medium height with an attractive face.

'Hello, my name is Comfort. I come to visit Emily sometimes.'

He took the hand and shook it. He knew his handshake was limp as his mind busied with questions.

Emily sat on the edge of the bed, her legs thin as twigs in a dress he remembered buying for her. She had a book in her hands and was trying hard to read it. She did not acknowledge him. Someone had tried to comb back the straw hair, but some stood in defiant tufts around her face.

'Can I see you outside, Mr Dean,' Comfort asked.

'Detective Dean,' he corrected. He stood indecisive for a

few minutes before nodding his head. There was something warm about her. He glanced back at Emily who was still clutching the book and followed the woman.

'I'm sorry that we have not met before. I am a member of the Light of the Mountain church and am here with the permission of the management.'

'They didn't seek my permission.'

'Emily asked to come to our church,' she said softly.

'Did she?'

'Her carers have brought her to our service and this is my outreach work for her. I came to share the scriptures with her.'

'Did you?'

'Detective Dean, your sister is in a deep spiritual bondage. She has recognised it and is willing to accept continuous prayers of deliverance.'

'I don't know what you're talking about. This will just confuse Emily. Please don't come back. If you step through my sister's room again I will have you arrested.'

She looked shocked.

'I do not think you understand, sir. We're trying to help Emily. We're the *good guys*.'

'You need to leave. I don't want to hear any more of this.' He made to walk away.

'You should understand. Your sister confessed to signing a satanic pact.'

Philip turned away from her and was surprised to see Emily, looking frail, standing in the doorway. 'Leave her,' he thought he heard her say. He walked to her and peered into her face.

'Emily. Did you say something?'

'Leave Comfort alone.' Her eyes looked clear as she gazed at him. 'She's helping me.'

He looked back at the woman watching him.

'Please go now, I want to talk to my sister.'

He watched her stride away with her head held high. He went back into the room with Emily. She was still clutching the book as she sat on her bed and turned her back to him.

'I don't want you involved in this kind of group. You've been through enough. What do you know about this church?'

Silence.

He sat there for a few minutes and then stood up. 'I need to pop out. I'll be back soon.' He went to the manager's office and knocked. A voice told him to enter.

'Hello, Detective Dean. I hope you're pleased with Emily's room. She's doing really well.'

The manager was a large-boned woman with milky skin and pink cheeks.

'There was a woman there.'

'Comfort? Yes, she's a befriender from a nearby Pentecostal church that does a lot of outreach work here. We have checked her background and cleared her to make visits if requested by our clients,' she said.

'I don't want her to visit my sister anymore. You know she's under strict psychiatric care.'

'Emily met Comfort at church and requested her visit. It's hard to explain, I do not go to church myself.'

'I'd rather my sister not go,' said Philip.

He heard her voice harden a little bit. 'Detective Dean, I have done this job for many years and it's hard for a lot to impress me. Emily's behaviour with staff in her previous homes has been abusive and challenging. She is showing none of this and that is remarkable. I would advise that if the church works for her, that we would be happy to take her there if she requests it.'

'I don't want her to come to see Emily again,' said Philip, his face hard as stone. 'She's vulnerable to anything. I don't think she's in a position to make a decision about what is good or bad for her now. I do understand that she has improved, but Emily seems to fall into influences easily. She had a boyfriend who was a terrible influence and that is what led her here. I don't want her to regress. If you don't stop that woman's visit, then I will speak to your director.'

'And I tell you that the ultimate decision is left up to Emily and not yourself. But, thank you for letting us know,' she said firmly. 'Now I'm afraid I have a meeting.'

***

Toks was in the computer room at the station, scanning the screen with a deep frown. It had been a few days since the Ezogies confession and they were still hunting for the child smuggler whom they now knew as Margaret Imafidon. She had fled her address in Thamesmead and was probably on the run. The uniforms had gone to the mental health hospital where she worked and were told that she had stopped working there about 2 months before. This woman must have handed Grace over somewhere. She was also wanted as part of a recently broken smuggling ring. Philip was on his way to talk to the detective in charge of the case while Toks continued to delve into the list of secret societies. Google and Facebook had been particularly helpful. She needed to narrow down the list.

She thought of Coretta, who had called her from Nigeria. She hoped her friend was being careful. She needed to understand that rules were different in Africa. Toks forced her mind back to her task as Google spat out her searches—The Yemoja Society, an international group that met yearly in Brazil and had large events that included dances and rituals. Her heart quickened because the UK chapter met weekly. She printed out the list of people that made up their governing body. Their leaflet said anyone was invited to join them. She called Philip immediately and passed him the information. He agreed to visit them later in the day. Tok's mind wandered to her son and church—both abandoned for this case. She would have to catch up with Bode properly soon. He never came to her room anymore. In the past he would wake her up and they would make breakfast. He loved pancakes. Things had gotten pretty screwed. She stretched her tired body and squinted at the screen. Another society had jumped up on her search—Etueje Society. This one seemed hard to understand. According to the data, they paid homage to all the forgotten Orishas of Africa. 'They did not believe in the Caucasian god.' All members on their list would have to be checked as well. She felt weary as she thought of the magnitude of the task ahead.

Thirty-Three

Coretta yawned and watched Richard's sleeping face as he gently snored. Melissa had accommodated them in a luxury bungalow on the sprawling grounds of her father-in-law's estate. Coretta pictured Melissa's other sumptuous homes in Mayfair, the Hamptons, and Dubai. She had given them a grand tour of the estate and pointed out a large swimming pool and tennis court for their use. Coretta had watched Richard with amusement as he looked around him in awe. This was leagues ahead of their already affluent life in London. The bungalow was nearly as big as their house.

The journey from the airport to the chief's estate had taken nearly two hours as they crawled through the tangle of cars that gridlocked the road as far as their eyes could see. They watched hawkers, young and old, aggressively selling sweets and mints, savouries, cheap Chinese imports of sunglasses and newspaper vendors with large hand-held wooden racks holding rows upon rows of newspapers and magazines. They continually tapped on their car windows or ran between the vehicles. Coretta didn't feel the heat, as the car was blissfully air-conditioned, but felt some guilt as rivulets of sweat ran down the faces of the hawkers onto their grimy clothing. She had explained to Richard that city-wide traffic jams were an accepted daily part of Lagos life. At the massive gates that led to the estate, they had been stopped for another check by armed uniformed guards who looked into the car and politely asked for their identification. Coretta handed over their passports to a heavily muscled guard with rippling biceps who had examined their faces against the photos before handing them back. She knew these were ex-soldiers hired by the chief who would not hesitate to shoot anyone that posed a danger.

The gates swung open to allow them through. Melissa's huge house was nestled far into the estate, near the main mansion. Tosin, as the eldest of the chief's sons, lived the nearest to his father. Chief Ogunladun's home was so huge that it had been likened to some minor palaces in Europe. It was rumoured to have more than 50 rooms and plenty of guest houses dotted all over the estate. Melissa had been waiting for them at their bungalow along with her daughter, Coretta's niece, Juanita. Coretta was pleased to see the girl and gave her a warm hug. At eight years old she was a mini-version of her mum. Melissa looked radiant.

'I'm so glad to see you.' She hugged them, her eyes shining with tears. 'I never see enough of my family, believe me.'

'Nice to see you, Melissa,' said Richard. 'This is incredible.'

'You get used to it. I will leave you to rest and then see you at dinner. Chief is hosting a social evening with visitors from the British High Commission and some others. Hope you'll be able to make it for my sake. I'm his hostess.'

'Oh?' said Coretta. 'What happened to all the wives?'

'He likes me to host ones like this,' said Melissa lightly. She looked elegant in a light pink *boubou* made from cotton and brocade.

'Aunty Coretta, how are Grandma and Grandpa?' asked Juanita.

'They send their love,' said Coretta, gazing at her fondly. It was a good thing that Melissa travelled with her frequently to England or they would have lost touch. 'I'll unpack your presents later.' She had deliberated over what to buy for a rich little girl whose parents travelled round the world in a private jet, and decided on some music vouchers and a few other girly things that Melissa told her Juanita would like.

Her sister had left them to their rest and promised to have them collected later for the gathering. Once she left, Coretta and Richard had fallen into bed.

Now awake, she raised herself on the soft bed and watched him. He was a bit red even though he had not been too exposed to the sun and the air in the room was cool from the air-conditioning. Coretta had helped him pack back in England and ensured that he took light T-shirts and lots of shorts. She rose and padded into a huge, cream marble bathroom with his 'n' hers wash basins, an ornate jacuzzi bathtub and a shower stall. She stepped into the shower, recalling that sometime ago Melissa had said she was redecorating the houses on the estate. She had employed an interior decorator and had flown materials into Nigeria from all over the world. Being the chief's favourite daughter-in-law, she was always given one project or the other to carry out for him. The shower pummelled the travel weariness from her body, and she sighed. She thought of her writing. The satisfactory conclusion of this trip would enable her to complete the first draft. She was pleased with what she had written so far—it made a compelling read. She still had not been able to reach Margaret Imafidon. The woman seemed either to have disappeared or was still avoiding her. She had the address of the supposed 'uncle', so perhaps he could solve a mystery that had baffled the whole of the Met police. After the invigorating shower, she checked her reflection in the mirror. Her newly-shampooed hair was tangled and her eyes, though still puffy with tiredness, glittered with excitement. She moved to the dining area and realised that lunch had already been set out. The delicious aroma of food made her stomach growl. Her mouth watered as she realised that Melissa had pandered to some of her seafood taste. There were large lobsters in hot sauce, fluffy brown rice, and prawn salads. She also saw some fried plantain. She suddenly felt ravenous and decided to wake Richard. Work could wait.

***

Philip had arranged to meet DS Sam Barn in order to get more information on the nurse, Margaret Imafidon. They were in a pub somewhere in Shoreditch. The man's face was already flushed with beer, which Philip knew was probably not his first or second for the day. There was something about him that Philip disliked. The man looked too smooth, comfortable and sleek for a police detective. Philip's face was expressionless as he watched him speak expansively about the operation that had exposed the smuggling ring.

'Same kind of stories. Smuggle them here as prostitutes to pay what is supposedly owed from the fare. And it's never over. Poor bitches. Become drug addicts and that's it. One was involved in a double murder from drug-induced rage.'

'A name came up in our investigation for little Grace,' said Philip. 'You're already looking for the same woman.'

'Who?'

Philip checked his notebook. He knew that DS Barn was only drawing it out for his own enjoyment as he had been briefed about who they were looking for.

'Margaret Imafidon.'

'Oh, the nurse. She seems to have disappeared but we'll find her.'

'What do you know about her?' asked Philip.

***

Toks was deep into her research on the Yemoja society. There was a lot of information online. Facebook was very productive! There were teachers, professors, nurses, builders, lawyers. The chief priest was a retired dance teacher. He had no record. Not even a parking ticket. The Etueje Society was not so clear-cut. Not all the members on the list showed up in the system. Some didn't seem to exist as there was nothing to show that they paid taxes or national insurance or were deceased. They just seemed to have disappeared. She would get them cross checked with the home office. She pinned down three names—Esme James, Steve Briggs and Bridget Folarin. Esme James was down as a teacher. How strange. She noticed there was some cross-over in the gods that some of the societies worshipped. The Yemoja Society claimed to worship the goddess of the sea but also revered *Orunmila* (a Yoruba god used for oracles). Etueje claimed to worship *Shango* and *Eshu*. That last name sent a prickling down her arms. Professor White had said that Grace could have been sacrificed to Eshu. They only had two days before the murder squad took over. Even more frustratingly, Venus was still missing. She had seemingly vanished, with no leads. They were no closer to solving either case. It was dispiriting.

She looked up when PC Walton entered the computer room. He looked distressed.

'We have a problem.'

She stiffened. 'What is it?'

'Your couple. The husband just tried to top himself.' Toks sprang up. 'He's been taken to hospital.'

'How?'

'Hanging. Thankfully the guv had said to place them on suicide watch or he wouldn't have made it.'

'What about the wife?'

'Seems fine to me.' His young face hardened. 'She's a tough one, that.'

Thirty-Four

Melissa sent a car round for Coretta and Richard much later that evening, even though the walk to the chief's mansion was just a few minutes away. She had called to say that it was best they arrived in a car so that they could look fresh. The mansion glittered like Harrods at Christmas – sparkling with hundreds of lights. Melissa had said the chief loved Britain in December and recreated the Christmas look at his home. Richard turned to Coretta and they grinned. It promised to be a fun evening! They were met at the front door by one of Melissa's party hostesses and led into a large room. As soon as they entered, Melissa waved them over. She looked stunning in an intricately styled, burgundy French lace blouse and a tight, bell-bottomed skirt. Her neck, wrists and ears glittered with diamonds.

'You look stunning,' Coretta said. Melissa always looked impeccable.

Richard was wearing one of his rare designer suits that Coretta had bought him. He hated suits and looked uncomfortable in this one. Meanwhile, Coretta wore one of the many gorgeous Nigerian outfits that her sister had gotten made for her. This one was of the same kind of lace material as Melissa's, but in a blend of silver and green. It made her feel sleek and sensuous. She had refused to tie the gele that had accompanied the outfit. Instead, Coretta let her hair flow down her back. She wondered if she should have agreed to wear it. Melissa's gele accentuated her swan neck and looked like a woven crown on her head. Coretta smiled inwardly as she knew she could never match Melissa's diamonds. She looked at the marbled floor and huge pillars with interest. As large as the room was, it felt cosy and this was due to the scattered rugs and comfortable chairs in the corners. The temperature was cold as soundless air conditioners hummed out chilled air. She was glad she had brought a light shawl. It was hard to believe, looking around, that she was in Nigeria. The diverse mix of people at this 'do' made it look like some international gathering in Vienna or Brussels.

'I'd better let you see Chief first,' Melissa said. They walked towards a thick group of people arguing in very loud voices. A short man in their midst argued the loudest. She had only met Melissa's father-in-law a few times at family do's – ones he could attend. Her parents seemed to see him more whenever he was in England, which was almost every month. He was a short, heavily set man, dressed simply in beige linen trousers and a top. She smiled as Richard eyed the loose-fitting outfit with envy. He had told her he would try to have a few of them made. The chief looked in his mid-60s, but she knew he was older than that—at least 75. He was full of vigour and power.

He saw them approach and smoothly handed the argument to another guest standing beside him.

'Thompson, you tell them what I mean,' he said heartily to a tall man with a clean-shaven head and sharp assessing eyes. He smiled at Coretta and she smiled back as she watched him gently take over the talk. Chief Ogunladun gave Coretta an appreciative look and she remembered that he was famous for his roving eyes. There was a rumour that he even had an Asian mistress. One of those beautiful Bollywood actresses flown secretly to Nigeria in his private jet and back home, richer. His wealth was endless it seemed – oil wells, telecoms, shares in diamonds mines in lucrative African countries, he loved startups as well and had many wins with companies like Google, Facebook, Uber, Whatsapp.

'Melissa, why do you continue to hide your sister? Welcome to Nigeria, Coretta. I never see enough of you and hear of you only when you come to cause me trouble.'

'Hello,' he held his hand out to Richard. 'Both of you need to come to see me when I am in London. I hope you enjoy it here. This is your first time in Nigeria, isn't it, Richard?' His eyes gleamed. 'You're in for a treat. Don't mind all those international doom and gloom stories. We have our poorest people here, whom we all try to help, and you have your inner cities. You might not want to go back to England after you've stayed here. How long are you around till?'

'A week,' said Richard.

'Not enough time! You will have to come again. We have a lot of ancient museums scattered all over the country that would interest you.' He turned back to Melissa and smiled at her fondly. 'Melissa will take care of you. You must let me see you before you leave. I'm going to Greece and then China, but will be back before you go.'

He turned to Coretta and grabbed her hand. 'Come, Coretta. Come and tell me more about your books. We will find somewhere to sit.' He drew her to a side chair. Coretta was a bit flustered. She had never had to explain her work to him.

'How are your books doing?'

'They're fine, sir. Have you been following the news about the butchering of that poor little girl?'

'Yes. A big shame,' he said.

'Sir, can I ask you a question?' Coretta felt a bit bold but she could see she was already losing his attention.

'Would you be able to introduce me to Chief Folarin?'

Coretta could not believe the switch in the chief as he became still and eyed her.

'What are you up to young lady? Chief Folarin is a good friend and business acquaintance. Why do you want to meet him?'

Coretta felt uncomfortable under his warning gaze. It was like she was speaking to two different people. 'I'm compiling a book on wealthy philanthropists in Africa and was going to add you and him, if you both agree, to the book.'

'That sounds good. I am happy you have learnt that these are safer things to talk about around here. Speak to Melissa and she will remind me. I can always speak to you when I come into London. I know you will enjoy your stay.' He held her hand briefly then stood and immediately joined another group. Coretta stared after him in fascination, then started as she realised that the man Thompson had been standing near them and might have overheard their conversation. He smiled at her.

'May I sit down?'

She nodded. He was wearing a narrow, baggy top and trousers made of brushed cotton. His musky aftershave wafted to her nose. He was very attractive and that disconcerted Coretta. Her job was male oriented and she met more men than women, many of whom were attractive. It had never been a problem as there was no one for her but Richard. That had been the case since they met at University in their 2nd year and they had been together for 15 years since. She screwed her eyes slightly as she gazed at Thompson. He needled her a bit. Standing there and listening to their conversation was sneaky and yet her breath caught slightly at his strong presence.

He gave her a slight smile. 'Sorry, I overheard your conversation with the Chief. It was not intentional.'

Coretta nodded and said nothing. Silence always worked to her advantage, but she seemed to have met her match. Thompson sat comfortably and looked out at the clustered groups of people. After about five minutes she sighed inwardly. Now she would have to ask him some questions.

'So, you heard myself and Chief talk? It couldn't have meant anything to you.'

'It did, though.'

'Shall we introduce ourselves again?' Coretta extended her hand. 'I'm Coretta Davies, nice to meet you.'

He took her hand and grinned, revealing strong white teeth. 'Coretta Davies. Wow! The true crime author. I have all your work at home. How do you do it? How do you get into all those worlds?'

'A bit of craziness. Anyway, you haven't said who you are and what you do.'

'I am Thompson Ighodaro, a media analyst. I own a tech company that supplies news all over the world.'

Her hand was still enveloped in his large one. He let go. 'I can tell you a bit about Chief Folarin if you want.' Coretta's heart leapt. 'But not here,' he said, looking around.

'Walls have ears. Shall we meet tomorrow at my work-place? It is on the outskirts of Lagos. I can send my driver to pick you up.'

Coretta swiftly rearranged her plans in her head. She was meant to head to Benin the next day, but this was a big fish to be caught. She could postpone her trip for a day and hear what Thompson had to say about the elusive Chief.

'That's fine. I'll expect your driver,' she said.

He stood up. 'Be careful around everyone, Coretta. Most especially your father-in-law. My driver will come at 12.' She watched as he walked away, lithe as a panther. Melissa bore down on her.

'Coretta, I saw you talking to Thompson Ighodaro. He just went through a second divorce. Stay away from him, he is dangerous to us women!'

Coretta giggled. 'I'm meeting up with him tomorrow. His driver's coming to collect me around twelve.'

Melissa stared. 'He's a charmer. I know you're faithful to Richard, but Thompson is a different breed. He's a seducer and very rich. That media house of his is worth plenty of money, and I don't mean Nigerian currency.'

'I can look after myself,' Coretta preened.

Melissa laughed and hugged her sister. 'I prefer you doing this than chasing dangerous criminals! Imagine the trouble you put me through last time!'

Coretta hid a smile. *You don't know the half of it, Melissa.*

She thought about the two names in the book that Margaret had given her. That uncle in Benin and Chief Folarin. There had to be a connection there somehow and she would get to the bottom of it.

Her sister's voice brought her back.

'Tosin was held up but he will join us soon. Coretta, do you really need to go to Benin?' she said, eyeing her anxiously.

'I'll go in two days if that's ok by you. Richard needs to go to Unilag every day. He's working with a professor of Anthropology on one of his researches.'

'I will see almost nothing of you two!' Melissa looked dismayed and almost close to tears.

'Once I get this trip to Benin out of the way we can have fun.' She tried another tactic. 'I told Papa I'd like to meet Chief Folarin and he said he would arrange it with you.'

Melissa watched her. 'What do you want with him?'

Coretta grinned. 'Believe it or not I'm trying to compile

a journal of African Philanthropists and his name came up. I will be interviewing Papa as well.'

Melissa looked relieved. 'That's easy. I'm friends with his fifth wife. Her name is Bisi. I could ask her.'

Coretta giggled. 'Did you say fifth?'

Melissa grinned. 'Yup. Chief is loaded. Worth billions,' she whispered. 'Bisi is stunning, and a smart girl to boot. There's a 40-year age gap but that hasn't stopped her. She has him wrapped around her dainty little finger. I can get her to speak to him. She has a charity do tomorrow if you want to come.'

Coretta looked down in thought. She was already post-poning her trip to Benin by a day. If she saw Chief Folarin what would that achieve? She could not ask him directly if he was behind cultism and trafficking, but Thompson Ighodaro might give some solid info. Although, what was he after? He could not be meeting her out of the goodness of his heart. Richard joined them. He looked relaxed and that pleased Coretta.

Melissa turned to him. 'Richard, you can use the car and driver that I've arranged already. Coretta, I'll arrange for a car that can travel the road to Benin and back.'

'Can't I fly?'

'Coretta, I thought I was coming with you to Benin,' interrupted Richard.

'If you follow me, love, then you'll miss some of your vital research time. You go to University of Lagos and I'll sort out Benin. I'm going in two days.' She was glad he didn't argue.

Melissa looked from one to the other. 'I'll try and find out about flights, but if you go in a car then I can send you with a driver and armed escorts. I can't allow you to travel without that. Nigeria might be fun, but kidnapping and armed robbery is real. You'll have those escorts wherever you go. The same for you, Richard.'

She looked around the large space. 'I'd better circulate and be the hostess. Let me introduce you to an interesting group, Coretta. They are some of the most popular film stars we have in Nigeria. By the way, do you watch Nigerian films?'

Coretta shook her head. 'Then you're missing out on Nollywood. Go on YouTube and catch up on some there. Come, Richard, do you want to meet our British High Commissioner?' She led them away with the slit in her skirt showing off smooth legs and heeled sandals.

Coretta felt her stomach clench with excitement. She might get some answers at last.

*****

The next day she was up bright and early. While Richard slept like a baby, she went on her MacBook and did some work. Her story was shaping up, but if she was honest with herself she had nothing solid yet. Everything seemed like hearsay and whispers. To make it work she needed some evidence and inside information. She really needed whatever Thompson was going to tell her and she hoped it wasn't going to be a waste of time. She was dressed by the time Richard woke up. She hugged and kissed him knowing she was softening him up for what she was about to tell him. He knew her and quickly sat back, watching her with a smile.

'Ok, spit it out, wife of mine!'

'Richard, I met a chap yesterday that is going to give me background info to what I'm after. His driver will be here soon.'

Richard nodded. 'Just be careful as always. Do you want me to come with you?'

Coretta hid her expression carefully. *No way!* 'No, darling. I'll be fine. I just wanted you to know. I'll be picked up soon but I think your driver is already waiting to take you to your professor. Why don't you have a shower and get ready?'

Richard nodded, watching Coretta. She definitely did not want him to come. She had been too careful in her answer to him, so it meant she was very excited. He would hold his breath till she returned. Coretta had set her rules long ago when it came to her work and she had deserved all the prizes she won, but it would never stop his anxiety when she was on a dangerous quest.

'Is he tall, dark and handsome? Has he got his sights set on you? If he has, let him know he's treading on dangerous grounds.' He grabbed and kissed her.

Coretta thought of Thompson Ighodaro's shaven head, musky aftershave, and supple steps, then shook her head. 'He's no match for you, darling.'

She heard the rumble of a car outside and opened the door. The heatwave almost sent her scuttling back inside. Parked in front was a white Lexus, with a uniformed driver behind the wheel and one of Melissa's security people seated on the passenger side.

'Hello, madam Coretta,' greeted the driver. 'I have come to collect you to Professor Ighodaro.'

Professor? Hmm. 'Thank you,' said Coretta. She looked at the security guard. He was a tall, angular man and reminded her of a razor blade, ready to cut when required. Casually dangling down his thigh was a Glock. Coretta knew her guns and this was a 9mm with a suppressor. She hid a shiver. It could shoot 10 rounds in a second.

'My name is Edwin,' he said. 'I am to escort you today.'

Coretta nodded. 'Thank you. Just give me a minute and I'll be out.'

She went back inside and saw that Richard was preparing to have his shower. She gave him a quick peck and collected her bag. 'I'm off, darling. Have a good day and wish me luck!'

He kissed her. 'Good luck. See you later.'

***

Toks was shocked by Mrs Ezogie's changed appearance when the woman was brought to the interview room. She had asked to speak to Toks and no one else. She was gaunt, with lifeless eyes and twitching hands. It still did not stop her from demanding information about her husband.

'How is my husband? I hope you people have not done anything to him.'

'Do you?' retorted Toks. 'Your husband is in capable hands

and will be looked after in hospital.'

Toks asked her if she wanted her solicitor before carefully turning on the recorder and video. 'I need to ask the questions now—you did ask to speak to me.'

She made sure their eyes met as she asked, 'What really happened to Grace?'

'We did nothing to Grace. We gave her to that woman, Margaret, to take back to the village for us and she did not do it.'

Her eyes filled with tears. 'Now, my poor niece has been killed in this terrible way and they're blaming us.'

'We're gathering evidence to link you and your husband to Grace's death.' Toks continued to look at her. 'You might never see your children again, let alone contact them. You are seen as child killers.'

The woman started to sob loudly, with a nose that slowly dripped mucous. Toks passed her a tissue and held her breath.

'Margaret said that there were a lot of people who were desperate to adopt orphans like Grace. It was too much for us: our three children and this little girl. She was a very strange girl. She would not talk, she would just stare at you with these eyes. My children were scared of her, you must understand. Margaret said there are people desperate for a child and they cannot get one to adopt because the procedure is too long. She took Grace away…'

Toks was on the edge of her seat, not daring to breathe.

'She said that Grace would go to a good white family. They would look after her.'

'Is that why you tortured her? We saw her burnt palm and broken fingers. You made her suffer! How much did Margaret give you?'

The woman looked down at the table.

'It was not because of the money. She said that the people she will give Grace to will look after her very well. They paid £10,000. She gave us £7,000 and took £3,000. Grace was supposed to have a good home. She would have suffered if we sent her back to the village.'

'You think so? You think what happened to her now is better than being in the village?'

'I don't know why they did this to her. They must be bad and evil people.'

'And you see yourself as good?'

The woman glared at Toks. 'You say you're Nigerian. That girl was a witch. Yes, she was small. But she caused havoc in my home. We had to do something!'

'So you tortured her. You have no proof of giving her to this woman. We have to assume you killed her. We also spoke to your children and they say they miss their cousin. They did not say anything about being scared of her.'

She looked defiant again. 'What do children know? One minute they are scared, the next they are friends!' Then the defiance vanished and she gripped the edge of the table. 'I miss my children. You have to believe us. This is what happened. You have to find Margaret. She did something to Grace. She put us in this situation. Please find her.'

'Is there anything you can tell us about her?'

Mrs Ezogie closed her eyes and then opened them. 'I only knew her slightly through her sister who attended our church. The sister is in jail. Maybe you should visit her. I think her name is Ukeria. Margaret also has some children somewhere.'

'We contacted the sister in jail and Margaret's children. They know nothing about where she's gone.'

'All we wanted was to give Grace a better home.'

'You abused her then sold her!'

The woman looked wounded.

As Toks watched her being led away, she found it hard to pity her. They had abused and sold the little girl for £10,000 and the poor thing had ended up being butchered. Just then it clicked in her brain that the first time she had heard the name Margaret Imafidon was from Coretta. She was the woman who gave her the contact in Benin. These people were smugglers and possibly killers, so Coretta would be in danger if she went. They could kidnap her.

Toks urgently needed to contact her.

***

Philip watched Emily stand against the wall and stare at nothing. Her body had shrunk even further and she looked like an old woman. He walked to her but she did not acknowledge or seem to recognise him. He could feel her emptiness. It was hard to explain, but he could feel the hollow where she should be. She was slipping away from him. He was losing his sister and he felt like lying down and crying. This was it, after all the years of struggle. He reached out and held her hand. She made no move to resist. Her fingers fluttered like bird bones in his hand.

'I promise, you'll get better soon,' he whispered to her. She still stared away from him with the lifeless look on her face, but he felt the tremor of her fingers. 'I will make it better.'

'You said send her away, so I did, but I want Comfort back.' Her voice was flat and toneless.

'Pardon?'

'Comfort. She knows what to do.'

He wracked his brain. Comfort? His mind cleared. *The church woman.*

He tenderly bent towards her. He could not believe they were having a conversation.

'It's good you sent her away. She would only have made things worse for you. She'll be like Austin. The doctors will help you get better. I don't trust any of that at all.'

'I want Comfort.' She finally looked at him and her eyes looked alive for a few seconds.

'Then send for her. I'll not get in your way,' he said, gently. 'Let me go and see a staff member. See how they're looking after you.'

He carefully let go of her hand and started to walk away. He looked back. She had not moved an inch.

Thirty-Five

The Lexus slithered through the dense Lagos traffic like a mamba in a jungle. The road was almost locked, with cars lined up for miles while Okadas, motorcycle taxis heavily laden with passengers, wove between the traffic. Coretta had never imagined you could pack 4 human beings on a motorcycle ride, but the Okadas defied anyone's imagination. They sliced through and Thompson's driver, seeing openings in traffic that she could not imagine a car could fit through, followed. Once they left the traffic behind, they coasted down the Lagos expressway to the outskirts of the city. Coretta did not feel much alarm. Melissa's security, whom she secretly nicknamed *Mr Glock,* was on alert beside the driver and she could see that, like all the other escorts, he was ex-army. They drove through a long stretch of road lined by dense forests. It took another half hour before they emerged into a landscaped town. It was all probably a private estate. They drove through a massive gate so high she imagined it matched the biblical height of King Solomon's temple gate in the bible. The houses were a mix of large duplexes and bungalows. It looked really pretty, but Coretta wondered how they managed security in such a dangerous environ as Lagos. The car settled in front of a huge, square glass building.

'We're here, ma,' said the driver. He came out and jumped 'round to open her door. 'The professor is waiting for you inside.' As he led the way, a door opened and Thompson stood grinning at her. He was dressed in a loose white baggy top and trousers.

'Welcome to Tropical town. I hope you like what you see. Come on in.'

He led the way proudly and Coretta saw that this must be his media empire. The building housed large open plan offices busy with staff. Most sat with headphones behind flat screens. It looked like a small stock exchange floor. Coretta relaxed. He led her to the back and opened a door to a lounge area with clear glass doors that showcased the view of tropical trees and landscaped lawns, leading to a set of raffia chairs with a cane centre table.

'Hope you like our setup,' he said.

'I do,' said Coretta, impressed. They sat down and he smiled at her again.

'Coretta, I feel as if I know you.'

She arched an eyebrow at him. He had a broad sculpted face and she realised that even with the loose top and trousers he exuded strength and intelligence. 'I had no idea you were a professor.'

She had done some background checks on him and they hadn't said anything about him being an academic.

'That was a recent thing.' He shrugged. 'I teach business and economics in Lagos business school and obtained my professorship that way.'

'So,' he looked at her, 'can I offer you anything to drink.'

'I'd like some juice, please,' she said, before diving straight into the purpose of her visit. 'What do you know about Chief Folarin?'

Thompson tapped his head and smiled. 'I told you I have read all your books. I hope you don't take offence at this. How do you do it? You are so small and dainty. I had imagined a macho, feminist fighter with all guns blazing.' He paused. 'You do have all guns blazing, but packaged nicely.'

Coretta smiled. 'I don't take offence. Thanks for reading my books. I admire what you have done as well. You started out on the internet with blogging on current affairs around the world. How did you turn it to this?'

He smiled. 'One thing led to another. I saw a gap in the market and took it. The big media companies were so busy reporting the big news that they did not focus on small, good quality news content which actually interests people. When I started collating this, I realised there was something to it and then partnered with a guy that was great at all the technology. Now we produce web services all over the world for the big media houses and quite a few businesses. I love being based in Nigeria, providing the service and not having to worry about living in the 'so-called' first world and all its pressures. We hand-pick the best graduates from local universities and train them. It works for everyone. Now, to your direct question about Chief Folarin. The reason that I preferred to talk in my environment is that I do not have to worry about what I say here and I trust you enough to tell you all I know.'

'Why, though?' The words came out of Coretta before she could stop herself.

He sighed. 'Coretta, I have a confession to make. Chief Folarin was my father-in-law. My ex-wife's father.'

Coretta was shocked. 'You were married twice though.'

'Yes. My first wife. I was close to him, but no longer so. I cannot investigate him, but I can give you as much information as I can. No catch. I don't believe that you can do anything with what I am about to tell you. The chief is very powerful and we have no proof.'

Coretta bit her lip. 'Would I be able to use this in my book?'

'That is up to you. You will have no proof and could be sued for defamation of character. However, you can write it in such a way that allows your readers to know how far you went in your investigation and let them know you couldn't get more than that.'

Coretta sighed. 'Okay, tell me.'

***

Toks called Philip but only got his voice mail so she left a message about Mrs Ezogie's confession. He called her back and told her to meet him at an address in Brixton. She thought of Bode and how she still had not been able to catch up with him.

He had been a bit moody and she felt bad that she couldn't even stay around long enough to tease whatever was on his mind out of him. Fortunately, Femi was back in London and they were meeting up. Maybe spending time with his father would help. She couldn't believe she was even thinking that way now. As soon as she got to the street in Brixton, she realised it was a crime scene. The whole area vibrated with the energy that uniformed police officers bring with them. She was not looking forward to what she would find here. She approached the two officers standing at the front and showed them her warrant card. She thought of Coretta. She had called her without success, but left her a long message about the obvious danger of going to someone recommended by Margaret Imafidon. Hopefully, she would have picked the message up and cancelled that trip to Benin. They had contacted the head of Nigerian police and told them about a child trafficking ring possibly operating out of Benin. That should start them off on some kind of investigation, Toks thought. The officers waved her in and she steeled herself against what she might witness. *Grace's missing torso?* She entered the house and smelt the sickening odour of death and blood. Philip was standing in the hallway chatting with another man. They turned when they saw her coming. He looked tired but alert.

'Not a good sight, Toks,' he grimaced

'The torso? Whose house is this?'

He shook his head. 'Not the torso.' He turned to the tall man beside him. 'This is DS Barn and it's his crime scene. The vic here is Margaret Imafidon.' Toks studied the other man.

He had a cocky, confident kind of air around him.

'Hello,' she said.

He nodded.

'We've been after her for weeks, but someone decided to splatter her all over the kitchen floor. This house belongs to her but it's in a different name, that's why we didn't know about it. The body is in the kitchen on the left. SOCO have already been, so it's fine.'

Toks prepared herself and walked into the kitchen. It looked like an abattoir. The headless thing that laid crouched on the ground did not look human, except that she could see the legs and hands. Dark pools of stagnant blood spread out like a pond. When she looked up, she gagged. The head with a grim mouth and closed eyes was attached to a ceiling fan slowly revolving over the corpse. She rushed past the two detectives and, once outside, gulped down the crisp fresh air. She did not feel like going back in.

***

Coretta watched as Thompson seemed to prepare himself to talk. 'I am a Benin man and of a royal household. I grew up with rituals because that is my culture. I am a Christian now, but my family and life was rooted in tradition and cults. We had our household gods; every traditional Benin household has a hut that houses altars for the different gods that protect us. That was how it was, and even when I came back home on holiday from my study in Britain I partook in all the rituals for

Olokun, the goddess of the sea, and other gods of my father's household. That was what strengthened us as a family. My father believed in the protection of his children and household in the traditional manner. As the first son of my father, I was taught and inducted into all the different cults that he belonged to, and this was where I met Chief Folarin. He and my father belonged to a cult that believed in the killing and shedding of new blood. Blood that is not tainted. Innocent blood. Every meeting we had resulted in the murder and sacrifice of a captive child. It did not mean anything to me. It was a means to an end.'

Coretta sat in disbelief, still as a statue. She needed him to finish his terrible story.

'Between my father and Chief Folarin, they arranged for me to marry his daughter, my first wife and the mother of my two children. It was a big society wedding full of men of the land who had grown powerful on the blood of the innocent. They are the brotherhood and you could not touch them. You still cannot touch them. The police and every fabric of our government has a member of this Brotherhood in power. Coretta, I am telling you that they know you are asking questions, they regard you like a child and know you will not gain anything. Besides, your father in law is part of it. They will leave you alone. If they believe you are too irritating or are too close, your father-in-law will ship you back to England and they will ruin you. But I don't think you could ever be a threat to them. Anyway, my father died and I discovered Jesus Christ and left all that behind. In revenge, the Brotherhood took their wealth away from me and my family. My mother passed away and the rest of my siblings accepted their judgement. We had to fend for ourselves. I discovered that I had a knack for blogging and created my own world. They left me alone because I promised that I would not reveal their secret to anyone. They, in turn, have said if I did, then my children would be gone. I have told you as much as I can, Coretta, but cannot say anymore. I can only tell you that the Brotherhood is international and headed in England by Chief Folarin. He might, or might not be, behind the death of the boy in the Thames, but you cannot prove it. Perhaps his death was to launch the brotherhood in Britain. They have a lot of members now, but it operates like a cell. In order to ensure that they build its powerbase in blood, they traffic children all over the world—some for cults and others to warped creatures in Europe that would pay the highest money for an innocent child. I am letting you know that a child successfully smuggled in Europe could fetch up to £100,000. They harvest organs, use them for dark arts, and also service paedophile groups. My former father-in-law is behind it, but there is no trail back to him. None, Coretta.'

'You seem to have told me a lot.' Coretta's voice was almost a whisper.

He shook his head. 'I have given you a tip of the iceberg. If I told you all I knew my family would be gone, I would be dead and you would be dead. It is too deep. What I suggest you do in your writing is hint at this, but no names. I know you are going to Benin tomorrow.'

Coretta started. 'How do you know that?'

He smirked. 'It's not magic. Security teams talk amongst themselves and I have a few informants planted amongst them. I did not develop a media house like this for nothing. On a more serious note, I will leave you to your investigation in Benin to come to your own conclusions. I do not want to influence anything.'

Coretta was silent as she took it all in. 'Thank you, Thompson. You have opened my eyes and you did not have to do this.'

'You're welcome, Coretta. I hope that you will return the favour one day.'

She nodded vigorously but swept her hands up. 'Absolutely. But I don't imagine you need me.'

He brought out two of her books with a flourish. 'I would be honoured if you could sign these for me.'

'I'm flattered,' she said. She took out her pen and signed the books.

***

On her return, she told Melissa that she would follow her to Madam Folarin No 5's charity do. She was filled with trepidation, especially in the light of Thompson's story. Could she even trust the man? She might finally be meeting the chief, but she would have to walk on eggshells in light of what Thompson had revealed to her. How do you suspend belief, thought Coretta, as she looked around her. Richard had opted to stay in to prepare for another meeting with his professor friend. The Chief's estate was almost identical to Melissa's father-in-law's, except this was almost twice the size. They had arrived at a gate swarming with security guards who had meticulously checked their invitation. Coretta was surprised to see her picture on an iPad held by a security guard with eyes cold and guarded as a viper's.

'Sit still,' Melissa hissed at her. Coretta went rigid as the guard brought out a scanner and swept it over her face. A green tick appeared on her picture on the iPad. He did the same to Melissa. Coretta shuddered. Once this was done, he waved their driver on and they drove through to a huge space full of expensive cars.

They had both been quiet in the car, as Melissa said they never spoke in front of the staff and it allowed Coretta to reflect on their earlier conversation.

'I like Bisi Folarin because she is not only beautiful but has a brilliant mind,' Melissa had said.

Coretta arched her eyebrow. 'Really?'

Melissa nodded vigorously. They were in her house and her room. She was wearing a floaty, gold gown from some Italian designer that Coretta could not remember and had offered Coretta another gown. They had both laughed as it would have been too big. Coretta wore a long white gown from Karen Millen. It was a classic look that she brought out with some jewellery and a pair of silver Jimmy Choos. Melissa loved the dress.

'Really. She's from a wealthy home,' said her sister.

'So, what is she doing being married to an old man with four wives?'

'Love,' said Melissa, simply. 'He wooed her and she fell for him.' She saw the sceptical look on Coretta's face. 'I know we have a lot of trophy wives here. It's a patriarchal society and some of the girls only have their beauty to trade for status, but Bisi was wooed by Chief Folarin and agreed to marry him. She actually went to Oxford and heads a large arm of his business.'

'Ok, Melissa. I find it all hard to understand, but if she's happy then that's what counts. The question tonight is, am I able to speak to Chief Folarin?' She felt a tingle just saying his name. If only Melissa knew, but there was no way she could share what she had learnt from Thompson with her sister.

'Bisi said he would make an appearance and she'll introduce you.' She looked at Coretta. 'I'm sticking my neck out for you on this because of the philanthropic angle. Chief Folarin has a few foundations, especially orphanages around the country, and would like to give them international exposure.'

Coretta quickly looked at the ground, then bent and pretended to do up her shoe as she felt her heart thump. *Orphanages!* Could it be as simple as that? This man had access to an endless number of children through his orphanages. Who would know if a child never reached an orphanage and was redirected to his trafficking ring? She wondered why Thompson did not mention this. When she straightened she looked into Melissa's eyes and said, 'I'm interested in the orphanages.'

Melissa had nodded happily. 'That's good. Let's go.'

And now here they were, in the lion's den. They stepped out in front of a large, Romanesque style building with marble columns. Society men and women in lavish, traditional outfits trooped inside. Standing close to the entrance was a beautiful young woman dressed in Valentino, with a mane of gold tinted hair extensions and strappy Jimmy Choos. Bisi Folarin warmly embraced Melissa. She whispered something into her ear and they both giggled. Melissa pulled Coretta forward.

'Bisi, meet my sister, Coretta. She's an award-winning writer and is compiling the philanthropic book I told you about. She thinks Chief would be good for it. Our Papa is definitely part of it.'

Coretta felt like a fraud. In fact, she felt like Judas. Was it right for her to use her sister's connection to infiltrate high society in order to attempt to bring one of its members down? She felt Bisi's assessing look as her lips moved in welcome.

'Indeed, Chief would be very interested. Do you know who else you're featuring in this book?'

Coretta nodded. She reeled off names of African billionaires, male and female: 'Dangote, Alakija, Masiyiwa, Oppenheimer, Danjuma, Chief Oguladun.' She saw the satisfaction in Bisi Folarin's eyes.

'That is good. Chief Folarin will definitely want to feature in this. Your sister is a very good friend, so I trust you.' She smiled her first genuine smile at Coretta.

She felt momentarily guilty but thought of the innocent children, and Victor, and instead simply said, 'Thank you.'

They walked through a marble colonnaded courtyard with

golden statues and showering fountains, to a huge space of glittering marquees and lights. It reminded Coretta of functions in the White house, all pomp and pageantry. There was a stage with musicians playing in the background, a pianist on the side and a full orchestra of music. To her shock, she recognised some international stars from America, a former United States president and a former British prime minister. It was then that Coretta knew that not only was Melissa moving within the highest circle, but Thompson Ighodaro was right. She was in way over her head. She would need to get Toks and give her this information. It was up to the British police to continue this. She would talk to the Chief briefly, but would keep it to no more than five minutes, with another appointment booked for a future date. Did she want to write about philanthropists in Africa? Maybe, but she knew that was not what interested her. She looked up as she realised there was someone towering over her. It was Thompson Ighodaro, and the look she caught in his eyes made her shiver. It was pure desire and admiration. He masked it quickly and smiled at her.

'Why am I not surprised you are here?'

She smiled back and said in a whisper, 'Why did you not tell me about the orphanages? What are you doing here?'

He smiled and steered her out to an open space on the ground. 'He is my father-in-law. Go back home to London, Coretta. This is bigger than you.'

'What does that mean? Are you saying all you told me were tales?'

He gazed into her eyes. 'I really, really like you. In fact, I believe that when I set my eyes on you I fell for you.' Coretta stood frozen. 'I know you love your husband, but think of me when you go back to your cold country. I will be here waiting.'

He looked at her. 'You have enough for your book.'

'I don't. An innocent little boy was killed. A little girl was butchered and scattered in London Parks. Should someone not fight for them?'

'The girl? That is not the brotherhood's style. And the boy should not have been found. The person behind it was punished. Did you look around the people here tonight? Former presidents and prime ministers of major countries. It is not as easy as you think. It is not black and white. It can never be.'

'So, what are you saying?'

'I have moved on. I believe in Jesus. Maybe, I'm just telling you to leave it this time. Let it go.'

He held her hands and she felt the roughness envelop her small ones. She had always disliked her child-like hands, but Thompson held them like he was holding a delicate piece of china. He pulled her close and she felt lips full and soft press down on hers one minute and the next gone. She held her breath.

'I had to do that,' he whispered in her ear. 'I want you to remember that I am here, always.' She watched as he walked away, his native outfit accentuating strong shoulders and legs that tread the ground like a lion in his jungle. Coretta could not think. No man had ever come close to her that way and none had kissed her since she met Richard years ago. Should she tell Richard? Could she tell him? She shook her head and went back to look for Melissa.

'Where have you been?' Melissa bore down on her. 'Chief is only here for half an hour whilst the presentation is going on. Bisi said to bring you down.'

Coretta followed her sister as they wove their way through the crowd. She had stopped counting the international stars and Arab money. Melissa came to a stop by Bisi Folarin who was standing by a tall old man of about Chief Ogunladun's age. He wore severe, black traditional trousers, and a baggy top with a strand of coral beads. Bisi gave Coretta a bright smile and introduced her.

He smiled at her with eyes as watchful and sharp as a hawk's. 'I'll be glad to talk to you. Bisi will get my PA to organise something soon. Philanthropy is at the heart of everything we do here. Children are the future.'

Coretta nodded. 'Thank you, sir.' She could not believe that this was he. The man that could have been behind the death of Alpha. What did she expect? That he had two heads?

Bisi clapped her perfect, slender hands and a woman in a suit came immediately. 'Jola, it is time. Chief will make his speech and we will then start the fundraising.'

Her sister turned to her. 'I hope this has helped.'

Coretta embraced her. 'Yes, it has.'

'Well then, let's enjoy the rest of the evening. There will be good food and drinks, and I will be dropping some thousands of dollars on Papa's behalf for this foundation.'

Thirty-Six

Philip had picked Esme James as the first member of the *Etueje* society to visit. One of the main reasons being, she lived in Highbury which was near enough. He had decided that depending on how helpful she was, he could then follow the rest of Tok's list chronologically.

He thought about the killing of Margaret Imafidon and felt disheartened. They almost seemed at a standstill. He arrived at Esme's street and gazed at her building, a block of about six flats carved out of a Victorian house, probably with young professionals in mind. It had a gravelled front yard and a huge chestnut tree that could offer cooling shade in the summer. He was looking for Flat 3b. According to Tok's information, Esme James was a 25-year-old former teacher who seemed to not be working and not claiming any benefits. He had called her as soon as Toks gave him the list and had told her he was doing some investigation on club memberships and she had said she would receive him. She had asked for his number and said she would check on him first. She must have done it quickly as she told him to come. Philip approached the oak front door and pressed the bell for 3b.

'Hello,' a soft voice greeted through the intercom.

'It's Detective Dean.'

'Come in.'

The buzzer sounded and the door opened. He entered into a communal hallway filled with bicycles and other bric a brac. He got to the top, climbing two at a time. A young, mixed race woman with a dark ponytail, wearing a neatly pressed cotton top and skirt with flat pumps, stood and waited for him in the doorway.

'Hello.' She extended a hand and gave him a firm handshake.

'Hello, I am Detective Dean.' He showed her his warrant card.

For a few seconds, Esme James regarded him and then said, 'Come this way, please.'

She led him into a small front room with large bay windows overlooking the street below.

'Please sit down. How can I help you detective?'

He cleared his throat.

'Thank you for seeing me. This is only a short meeting.'

'Can I offer you a drink?' He politely declined.

'No, thank you. I believe that you belong to the Etueje Society?'

Her hand went to her lips. 'Yes. But what has Etueje got to do with the police?'

'We just want to know more about you.'

'Have you gone to our website?'

'We have. We're updating our information on societies like yours and a few names that came up did not seem to have much information on them.'

'Like what?' she looked puzzled. 'Why are the police interested in any of our members? This is a waste of taxpayer's money.'

'What is the main purpose of your society?'

'We believe in the old African deities. Everything stems from Africa and we are all connected to that great continent. Christianity seems to have consigned these deities to the devil. We at Etueje believe in them and pay them the right homage. They all have their special functions just like the Greek gods, that's why there are so many.'

'Please name the gods.'

It seemed to Philip as if he had turned a light on in her as her eyes steamed with intensity. 'In Etueje you're allowed to choose any one of the hundreds of the African Orishas. I am a follower of Oya and Yemoja. Both goddesses.'

'Do you offer sacrifices?'

She laughed softly.

'No. We're not at all like that.'

'I need a contact for all of these people.' He reeled off the names.

'I don't know who they are. I haven't seen them at our meetings. We work in groups and come together only once a year. Members of my group worship the same goddesses as me. That's all we do. Pay our respects. We do not break the law. You'll have to track these folks yourself.'

She stood up and led him to the door.

'I'm meeting your leader today,' he said to her back.

'That's a good idea. Perhaps he can make you realise that what we're doing is no different from so-called 'Christianity'. We just allow our deities to appeal to God for us.'

'Thank you, Miss James.'

'Thanks for coming to see me. I'm always happy to talk about what we do, but I still believe you should be chasing criminals not religious societies.'

She opened the door for him.

***

Coretta could never lose the feeling of being watched by Melissa's guards. She missed her freedom in England. They were on their way to an orphanage. It was interesting that Soji, the driver assigned to drive them around, had offered to show her a children's home by someone known to his sister. So much for the workers not overhearing their conversation. Coretta thought hard before she decided to cancel her trip to Benin. She had paid £1.5K for two names and although it was a lot of money, it had flagged up Chief Folarin. Going to Benin to meet Margaret's uncle might not produce anything and could be dangerous. She saw some missed calls from Toks, but had decided not to call back yet. Her friend would demand too much explanation and everything still seemed to be covered in smoke. She knew powerful people were behind the killing of the little boy and understood a little of that, but what could she give to Toks? Maybe she could give her the name of Chief Folarin and let the police do some digging? Maybe they might be able to find something in England for he seemed impregnable here in Nigeria.

She thought of Melissa and felt a bit sorry for her sister. They hardly saw her husband Tosin, who seemed on permanent business travel. She remembered their earlier conversation about Melissa's art.

'Did you do anything about the art stuff you wanted to do?' Coretta had asked her.

Her sister's face had lit up.

'I've created a studio but the chief is keeping me busy.'

'He should use one of the wives,' Coretta said.

'He's got some well-educated ones, but he's a very clever man. If I do all his hostess work, then there is no talk of favouritism amongst them. It does leave me little time to do my own thing or dream my own dreams.'

'You'll have to look at it as a job and do some time management so you can work on your art,' said Coretta. 'How many wives has he got now?'

'Four, and lots of mistresses.'

She was jolted back to the present as the car slowed. They were behind a long line of traffic. The head of the guards, known as Captain by his men, hunched forward and whispered to the guard sitting by the driver. He had charmingly introduced himself to Coretta as James, but she could only think of him as Captain. He was a ruggedly handsome man but the saying 'the eyes are the windows of the soul' was true in his case, she thought. Behind his smiling face and polite courtesy, were eyes like black marbles that missed nothing. Melissa had told her that the guards were trained mercenaries from Sierra Leone. They sold their skills all around Africa and everywhere else that would have them.

'Is there a problem?'

'Nothing madam,' Captain said. He turned back and she saw him scan the road ahead as the tailback ended and traffic flowed as normal. The sweltering heat outside was unrelenting but she was cocooned in the air-conditioned car. She checked her tan. She had been careful with the sun and had urged Richard to do the same. They drove into a busy petrol station. She watched as child hawkers carrying wide trays laden with food ran around tapping car windows, and displaying their wares. The trays had bread of all shapes and sizes, fried meat, snail, pork, plantain, roasted corn, peanuts. She saw that some of the children were probably no older than six. Windows rolled down as passengers in other cars bought from the hawkers. It was all too much for Coretta when she saw a little boy running after a moving car to collect money for his loaf of bread. They drove out of the petrol station into another tailback. She looked at Captain, he was whispering rapidly into his phone and looking at the line of vehicles in front. She saw one of the guards from the Peugeot behind setting off at a trot. He passed their car without a backward glance.

'Captain, can you tell me what's wrong?'

Soji, the driver, nodded as if he approved of her asking

this question. He was a thin man with a lisp and Melissa had assured her that he was one of their best drivers.

'We want to check what is going on in front,' Captain answered.

Coretta looked at the row of traffic.

There was a rap on the window. It was the guard that had jogged past them. Captain wound down the glass and Coretta flinched as waves of heat hit her face.

'Yes?'

The guard was a tall, strong-muscled man. She could imagine him working out every day. His voice had a deep timbre. 'It is an accident, sir. They are trying to clear it. We're fine.'

Captain wound up the glass and Coretta saw he had visibly relaxed.

'What were you expecting to see, Captain?'

The man latched his brooding dark eyes on her. 'Armed robbers or kidnappers, madam. They are deadly people, and because they know there are more and more cars with escorts like us, they descend on the roads in large numbers like vultures.'

Coretta tensed. 'Like, how many could they be?'

Captain smiled revealing large teeth with sharp molars. They marred his looks.

'Sometimes 30 or 40, and they kill on sight.'

'How much longer will it take us, Soji?'

'About half an hour, madam.'

She liked his driving skills. His hands were steady on the

wheel and so far he had not given in to many of the mad drivers that they had encountered since she came to Nigeria.

***

Philip had phoned Toks to say that he had spoken to one Etueje member. She had tried to get more information about the ones not on record and realised that one of them, Bridget Folarin, was under diplomatic protection. She should have listened more carefully to Coretta when she was discussing her research because a few things she had said were starting to cross over into this investigation. Fortunately, she had a habit of jotting things down at the end of the day and so had been able to see that Coretta had mentioned a Folarin at some point. Could Coretta's address that Ukeria had given her be the same as Bridget Folarin's? There was no way to know as she could not reach Coretta. Ukeria was said to have died of a heart attack after being rushed from the prison to hospital.

Tok's phone rang.

'Hello.'

'Madam? Are you the police, madam?'

'Yes. Who is this?'

'I'm Fred. From the market. You said I should call you if those people should come and buy more pots.'

Her heart leapt.

'Yes. Did you manage to get their names?'

'They refused to write down their names, madam.'

'Oh,' she said, disappointed.

'They needed my help because they bought a big pot and plenty of small ones, so I said I will help them take some to the car. I have their car registration. Do you want it?'

Good man! 'Yes, please. Are they the same people?'

'Yes. The white man and woman.' He then slowly read out the registration which she wrote down.

'Thank you. Thank you so much.'

Thirty-Seven

Toks felt they were finally getting somewhere with their investigation as they drove to affluent Hampstead to interview the registered owners of the car, a retired couple, Patricia and John Hopper.

'John taught history at a prep school where Patricia was headmistress,' said Philip. 'Neither has a criminal conviction. Not even a parking fine.'

They arrived at the address and she eyed the little private dirt road that led to the house simply known as, 'The Darlington'. No number. It opened out to reveal a big house with a huge front lawn.

'We are stepping on a tightrope here, Toks. All we have is that they bought some pots from Brixton. Based on that we can't get a search warrant, so all we can do is talk. I called ahead so they're expecting us.' He gave her a weary sideways glance.

She did not tell him that she had dug up a plan of the Hopper's house and memorised the layout.

'If we find enough cause, then we will go get a warrant,'

he continued.

Toks thought about that long process. There was no way she could wait for all that. Venus was still missing, connected or unconnected to this, and they had not been able to tie more than child abuse and smuggling to the Ezogies. Those people were going nowhere but they must have accomplices. She experienced a buzz of adrenaline.

The front door opened as soon as they rang the bell.

A lady in her late fifties or early sixties welcomed them. Patricia Hopper was of smallish build, with a trim waist.

'Hello, officers. Come in.'

They entered a large hallway with walls of paintings. Patricia's ballerina shoes made no sound on the dark wooden floor as she led them straight into a cosy room with a printed rug, large comfortable chairs and paintings of Greek gods and goddesses. Zeus and his entourage of gods dominated a whole wall. It was incredible work. John Hopper joined them. He was as small as his wife, with white hair and pointy ears that gave him an impish look. They eyed Toks and Philip expectantly.

'Many thanks Mr and Mrs Hopper for agreeing to see us on such short notice. We have an ongoing investigation and just wanted to clear some things up,' Philip said.

'That's fine,' John Hopper replied. 'Please, sit down,' he indicated the settees.

Toks glanced at her phone and said, 'May I use your toilet, please? I also have to make a quick call.'

She avoided Philip's curious look. She had decided to do a quick check and nothing more.

'That's fine,' said Patricia as she stood up smartly. They walked down the hall and she pointed to a door on the left. 'Here you are.'

'Thanks.'

'Will you be fine getting back?' she asked.

'Yes, thanks,' said Toks.

As soon as she saw Patricia disappear into the front room she set off past the toilet and straight across the hall. She knew enough of the plan to aim straight for the basement. She ignored her pounding heart as she progressed. According to the plan, it was at the end of the hall. She went past a series of doors till she arrived at the last one. She opened it to see a yawning darkness. She felt around the entrance and her hand caught a light switch which she gratefully turned on. The place filled with low light. *Why do basements always have to look dark?* Her mind travelled to those countless horror movies with low-lit naked bulbs that go out as soon as the actor got to the bottom of the stairs. She looked down. It was a long way. She took one step after the other and felt a coldness drifting from below. It raised goose pimples on her arms. She could not hear anything except the sound of her footsteps. How long had she been away? Five minutes? She finally made out the bottom stairs in the gloom and looked up. The door at the top looked far away. She turned back to examine the large, almost cavernous space. It was filled with objects and furniture covered in white sheets. She spied a heavy looking metal door at the other end of the room and walked to it. It had a huge padlock. The door made no sense. It was not in the plan that she memorised. She knew then that she should turn back and go to Philip. Would this be enough for a warrant? Then she wondered where the door would lead. What if that plan was an old one? She rooted around a little purse that she hid in her jacket and brought out a pin. She should be able to open the padlock. Toks bent low in concentration as cold sweat trickled down her face. She was now out of time and needed to get back upstairs, but a stubbornness kept her at the door. Finally she heard the click as it opened. The door led into a narrow passageway with a musty smell. This was turning into a medieval adventure, she thought, as she noted the freshly painted white walls. She walked down its narrow length and stopped as a massive steel door confronted her. It looked impregnable and reminded her of a bank vault. She bent to give it a closer examination and jerked as a strong arm gripped her waist and another clamped itself to her mouth. Her brain screamed as she realised she had been foolish. Someone must have been hiding in the basement! Then the hands disappeared and before she could turn around and look at her assailant, she felt an excruciating, jarring pain to the side of her head and knew no more.

***

Philip looked at the couple keenly and glanced at his notebook.

'Please could you show me the pots in your garden? As I explained earlier, it will allow us to eliminate them from our list.'

269

He glanced at his watch. Toks had been gone five minutes. He stood up and Patricia did the same, then gave an annoyed sigh as she stared at Philip. He ignored her. He was very worried about Toks and needed to call her. 'Your toilet is just down the hallway. Let's find Detective Ade.'

John Hopper stood up. 'Sit down. I'd better go find her myself. It's a big house.'

'I'll call her,' he raised his phone. They turned to him and he realised they looked scared. He dialled and was dismayed when it went straight to voicemail.

'I'll go and look for her,' said John. Husband and wife exchanged looks.

'Careful, dear,' Patricia said to her husband.

'I'll come with you,' said Philip. *Where was she?*

John went up to him and Philip realised he looked terror-stricken.

'Detective, why did you and partner come in like this? The pots were just for gardening, nothing else.'

Philip decided not to mince his next words. 'Why are you scared, then?'

His phone rang and John Hopper jumped. He picked it up thinking it was Toks but it was Katherine.

'Hi, Philip, I've found something on the list you told me to check.'

'Go on,' he said, keeping an eye on the couple who were now holding hands.

'Are you already at the Hopper's residence?'

'Yes.' John and Patricia seemed frozen in place.

'You told me to track their background. They worked as foster carers about 10 years ago.'

'Ok?'

'One of their foster children was Steve Briggs. He's one of the untraceable people on the Etueje list,' she said. He looked at the couple and then all of the strands seemed to come together. He killed the call with a quick thanks to her.

'Where is he?' he asked.

John Hopper licked his lips. 'Who?'

'Where's Steve?'

The couple held each other's hands tighter and then Patricia began to sob.

'You should never have come. We could have managed.'

'I'm going to look for my partner. Is she in any danger?'

Patricia's sobs got louder.

'Where would she be?' he persisted.

He saw both looking down. 'Where is your basement?'

The man slowly walked outside and pointed to a door down the hallway, to the far left. Philip ran down and yanked it open.

***

Once Toks regained consciousness she realised she was lying on a cold, hard surface, unable to move. What had she walked into? They had been sure the Hoppers lived alone. What a terrible assumption. She tried to sit up but realised she could only move her head. A wet animal smell filled the whole space and she started to retch. She must be lying in an underground somewhere. *Was this a part of the basement?* She felt burning pains on her hands which were hanging down the side. She tried to raise an arm but could not, then heard footsteps. A face came into view and she tried to jerk away.

'Don't bother to struggle,' he said. She froze. The face was round, puffy, with deep-set eyes so distant they looked inhuman. She closed her eyes and started singing in her head. She tried to speak but her lips were stiff. *His voice. What was wrong with his voice?*

'It's no use. I helped you to relax with a little injection. I didn't want to tie you down. Now, just give up and listen carefully.'

She must give up, she thought. It was better. How could she have thought the voice was terrifying? Now it warmed her. It was not so bad now. She waited for him to speak.

'You're listening. Good. A life blood like yours is not pure. You are not an innocent, but it would still please him. I will slowly let it out and it will flow directly to him. Warm, alive and close to the earth. It was good he sent you to me. You are not an innocent but he will welcome your blood. When he has had his fill, then I will bathe in the rest. Your blood will bless me. Cleanse me. Well done!'

Toks felt a warm glow. *She was special.* His voice was so melodious. She must listen to him. She must. She wanted to pray. And the praise words flowed sweetly out of her. And then she felt piercing points of pain and screamed. It was a blast of arctic air on her body so cold it instantly froze her lips and she stopped feeling them.

'Shut up,' he snarled.

He hovered above her holding a shiny metal canister resembling a fire extinguisher. It continued to gush frozen air over her. She felt icy flakes covering her.

'Don't you dare pollute my sacrifice. I can finish you off in a few minutes with this if you continue.' He turned it off, went to a corner of the room, and threw something shiny over her. *An insulating blanket.* 'You try that again and I will sew up your lips. Do not foul the sacrifice with that. Better to give yourself up willingly. The cut will be coming soon to let out your life flow and you will welcome it.'

***

Philip ran down to the bottom of the basement. Still slightly breathless from his fast run, he walked to a steel door at the end of the large cold space. It was wide open and he could see a passageway. He entered it and, after a surprised glance at John Hopper following cautiously behind, walked forward. He had already called for back-up.

'You had better start telling me everything now,' he said to the man.

'We fostered him when he was a teenager and didn't know what he was. It's hard to explain. He just has this power to control people.'

Philip came to a stop and stared at an impenetrable barrier that ended the passageway—a locked steel door with a shiny smooth surface. Apart from a small keyhole, there were no door handles or anything else that he could grip.

He bent to look through the keyhole. It was dark. He turned to John Hopper. 'Where does this lead to? Where is he holding my colleague?'

'He studied structural engineering. He built this himself. It took him five years.'

Philip tried to bang on the door but only hurt his hand. 'What is this?'

'It's something like an underground bunker with reinforced steel. No-one can get in,' he said sadly.

'How did you manage to get this built without permission?' asked Philip.

'We did. We asked for permission for some extension and Stevie built this alongside that. That is where he's holding your colleague. I'm sorry.'

Philip tried to hit the door with his shoulder but it made no difference. Sweat ran down his face. He tried to find a handkerchief and failed, wiping some off with his hands.

'Why did you allow him to do this? How many people has he brought here?'

'He told us that he wanted to worship and sacrifice animals like the old ways. That it was even in the bible. King Solomon sacrificed 120,000 sheep in one go at one of God's temples. All we were required to do was to supply him with money, food, and run a few errands.'

'Like leaving pots in the park?'

'You don't know him. He can make you kill for him, if he

wants. It's like he's not human.'

Philip remembered his encounter with Austin. If he was something like that, then his heart ached for Toks. How many of these types of psychopaths were around? She would be undergoing ten times worse than what he went through in Austin's hands.

He turned around to face John Hopper.

'John Hopper, you and Mrs Hopper will be taken to the station for further questioning on the part you played in the murder of Grace and the abduction of Detective Toks Ade.' The man just hung his head. Philip led him out of the passageway just as he heard pounding feet and shouts. Backup had arrived. They needed to plan how they could save Toks's life. They had very little time and still had to understand the kind of maniac they were dealing with. John and Patricia had the key to his answer.

Thirty-Eight

Toks was fading in and out and knew that the drug the man injected into her was still making her drowsy. She could feel it. She prayed under her breath. He could see her. She could feel him beside me.

'You need to stop that now or it will end.' His voice drilled into her brain. It hurt.

'Do not contaminate my sacrifice. He is not a forgiving god. Give yourself willingly and He will take care of you for all eternity.'

He had described in excruciating detail what he was going to do to her. Her arms would be incised and her blood would feed the black mound of clay erected for his god. He had given her drops of water laced with vinegar.

'Just like that usurper, Jesus. So, drink His water. You are worshiping the wrong god. Worship my lord and let yourself go. Offer yourself willingly. Don't make me take your soul by force.'

She was cold, so cold. He had removed her insulated blanket and trailed a sharp, serrated knife over her chest. He hovered above her and she could see the spittle on the sides of his rubbery lips as he spoke.

'I could cut you up now. Take all your blood. Or hang you upside-down and drain you that way. Maybe I should do that.'

The tip of the knife rested over her heart. She thought of Bode and tears trickled down the side of her face. It was difficult to try and think. How could she get out of this? She must think of a way. She must pretend she had fainted.

'I could end it now and my sacrifice would be complete. Nobody can rescue you down here. We will be sealed in forever. I have left my Lord dead offerings scattered over the four areas of this foul town. How many people go to church now? How many believe? We're winning. Should I end it now?'

She made his voice fade into the background as she began to plan how to get herself out of this mess.

***

Philip, DCI Jackson and Supt Amos were standing in front of the steel door in the Hopper's basement.

'I fear that every minute we waste means less chance for Toks,' said Philip. 'The basement and garden have been completely altered by Steve Briggs to create an underground bunker. He used the Hoppers to run errands for him, including buying the pots that he used for the sacrifices.'

'What's your plan?' asked DCI Jackson. 'We take it that Steve forced Toks in there. How do we get her out?'

'An engineer has checked it. That door is as strong as a

bank vault. We cannot get her out, so we have to try and lure him out.'

'How?'

'I have spoken to the Hoppers again and got nothing from them aside from the fact that they've lived in fear of him for years and provided everything he's demanded.'

Katherine joined them.

'How do we lure him out, Philip?' asked DCI Jackson.

'This man operates in rituals and we know he has not performed the final one. Little Grace's torso is still missing. He has moved away from his pattern.'

'It's a shitty situation,' said DCI Jackson. 'The bastard has everything he needs in that bunker. We know he has a year's supply of clay pots, food, knives. The Hoppers have said that they have no means of communicating with him once he's down there. He's been known to spend weeks there. This is a man who disappeared from the system!'

'We'll cut off his electricity supply,' said DSupt Amos.

'Guv, that's a great idea!' said DCI Jackson, almost clapping.

Philip made the phone call to the electrician.

'We'll also see if we can get anything out of Esme James. The Hoppers confirmed that Esme visited Steve regularly. She is the link. We've gone to fetch her and Katherine can interview her.'

***

As their drive continued, Coretta wondered if she had been foolish in trusting Soji to take them to this orphanage he had fervently described to her. Could this be one of Chief Folarin's orphanages? Was he connected to this? She felt very jittery after all that she had heard but gave a brave internal shrug. She stole a glance at Captain's rigid face as he sat beside her in cold silence with a large hand tapping the Glock in his holster. He definitely had not approved of the trip but Coretta had told him it was one she needed to make and had carefully left Soji's name out. They had been travelling for twenty minutes and shuddered and bumped through potholes in untarred streets bordered by filthy gushing gutters. It had rained the previous night.

Soji slowed down and stopped in front of a huge dilap-idated building with patches of ancient peeling paints and windows boarded up with planks. Captain became alert and jumped out to open the door for her. The sun was a burning ball in the clear sky. Sweat beaded her face and Coretta brought out a handkerchief. She was wearing a sleeveless T-shirt and long shorts. Soji sidled up to her and whispered in her ears, conscious of Captain's eyes on them.

'Madam, this house is the orphanage. The woman here is not nice and sells the children. My sister used to work here. I want you to help them.'

'Why is nobody stopping her?' Coretta asked.

'Nobody know. She go to villages and everywhere to take children from poor people. Some, she will sell to rich, rich people without children. She is a strong *juju* woman.'

Juju. Coretta was becoming sick of the thing. Why was everything about *juju?*

They walked to the front door and Soji rapped on it. She could see that Captain was not happy at the driver taking control like this. *Tough.*

The door opened and a woman stood before them. Coretta was struck by her resemblance to Ukeria Imafidon. Could they be related? The woman opened the door wider.

'Good morning o, madam. My name is Mercy. Have you come to see children?'

Coretta returned her greeting and told her that they had.

Mercy looked at the men apprehensively. 'Only you and one person can come in. It will make the children afraid if they see all these men.'

'That is fine,' said Coretta.

She turned around and told Captain and his men to stay outside whilst she went in with Soji. After all, the driver had made her come here. She felt a firm hand detaining her and turned.

'Madam, I'm not happy about this. Where is this driver taking you?' asked Captain.

Coretta looked pointedly at her arm and he let go but still looked at her challengingly.

'I understand your concern, but I'm fine. We'll be back soon. If not, you have my permission to come in. This is just an orphanage.'

'Ok, Madam. I will give only 15 minutes before I come in. My job is to keep you safe.'

'Agreed.'

The woman led them in and Coretta was struck by how dirty the house was. The wide bare hallway through which she led them was gritty with sand. It seemed to lead to quite a few rooms which were shut, but from which issued cries of children. This place already reminded her of a Romanian orphanage she had been to back in her reporting days and over which she had wept when she came out. She felt her shoulders tightening with anxiety and anger. They saw a little girl of about four wearing a faded torn dress coming out of a room. Coretta approached her.

'Hello,' she bent down to the girl's level and was shocked at how emaciated she looked. The little girl ran off after giving Mercy a scared look.

'Madam,' said Mercy. 'I am the manager here. I will show you the babies. The babies are better. You want a child, isn't it?'

Her eyes had taken on a greedy glint. Coretta hid her disgust. They came to a closed door and the woman told them to wait before going inside. She came out and signalled for them to come in. She had not asked a single question about who they were or where they came from. Coretta was starting to believe Soji. They entered a large room filled with cots. The stink of faeces in the room was overwhelming and Coretta coughed. About ten babies, looking small and malnourished, lay in rows of two on dirt-encrusted mattresses. On a single bed beside the only large window in the room, sat a young girl of about fifteen. The babies only had on what appeared to be soiled cloth nappies. It was hard to tell their sex as some looked only a few months old.

'I get fine babies every day,' said Mercy from behind them.

Coretta had forgotten about her. 'Where do these babies come from?'

'All over, madam. All these young girls. They put them on our doorstep or police bring them. I try to give them good home.' She moved to one of the mattresses. 'See, this little girl. She's fine, o. She has light skin like you.'

To Coretta, the baby looked very fragile and delicate.

'We try our best but some of these children die. Her name is Angel. If you take her you will help her life.'

She looked so sincere that Coretta almost found it hard to relate her to the monster that was selling children. She looked at the baby again. She had dark curly hair, brown eyes and even in her malnourished state you could see how beautiful she was. *How long would she last here?* She would be perfect for her and Richard. She let herself dream. She could take her away from all of this. Give her a better life. She saw the greed in Mercy's eyes and gave her a hard look.

'How much?'

'One million naira,' she said without hesitation. Coretta looked at the girl again. What would become of her and all the children here?

'I'll come back.'

'Ok, madam, you can have her for N800,000. No problem.'

'I'll come back,' Coretta said in a harder voice. 'Madam Mercy, why is this place so dirty and the children not well looked after?'

The woman looked sad but Coretta detected the glint in her eyes. 'We have no money. Government are not helping us.'

'Madam Mercy, I don't understand it here. You don't know me and yet you want to sell me a child. This is not an orphanage. You are selling children and someone is killing them!'

The woman clapped her hand to her mouth and Coretta saw anger and shock there.

'You have to go! I was trying to help you. This is not your business. Plenty fine people come here to take children. I think you are like them. Who send you? Go, go go!'

She almost pushed them out with her body. Coretta walked out of the house with Soji trailing behind. This place needed to be shut down. Why was no one doing anything? It was when she got into the car and they were on their way that she realised something strange. Not one of the babies had cried whilst she was there. Not one.

Thirty-Nine

They had tracked and arrested all of the members of the society and questioned them. It emerged that Steve and Esme had broken away from Etueje ritual worshiping, which they termed too tame, in order to carry out their own form.

At the station, Esme James sat before Katherine looking soft and pliant. She was wearing a floaty white shirt and skirt—an outfit that would have been more suited to summer.

'We want to cut the bullshit and tell you right off, members of your society are in a lot of trouble,' she said.

'How come?' said Esme.

'Isn't Steve a member?'

Esme shrugged her shoulders indifferently.

'We know you have some relationship with him.'

She gazed scornfully at Katherine. 'It's a free world.'

'We need access to his vault. He's holding my colleague hostage and is a violent man. If you tell us now, then we might work out a deal for you.'

Esme looked angry. 'I haven't been charged and I've done no wrong. Steve is very secretive. I don't know much about his bunker. He would never reveal such information to anyone…'

'…except you, his partner,' said Katherine. 'You must have a code or key to get in. Hand it over.' Katherine extended her hand to Esme, who made to stand up.

'I don't have access. If you have nothing to charge me with then I'd better go. I don't enjoy wasting my time at a grotty police station.'

'You are not free to go. You are the partner of a man that has just kidnapped my colleague. You are linked to his secret society and the ritual sacrifice of a child. You are not helping me, so we will hold you till you do. Esme James, I am placing you under arrest. You do not have to say anything, but it may harm your defence if you do not mention when questioned something which you may later rely on in court. Anything you do or say may be given in evidence.'

Katherine stood up and signalled for a uniformed sergeant.

Esme seemed to lose her cool as she yelled curses at them. 'Useless fuckers. You have nothing on me. You have no right to hold me. I want to speak to a lawyer!'

'You can get a lawyer. That will be arranged for you,' said Katherine.

***

Toks thought she had died when all she saw was darkness. Then she heard the snarling, swearing voice in the background and kept her eyes shut.

'The fuckers! They've turned off my electricity supply! We

need light and air!'

She lifted her arms up in the dark and was grateful that she could move them now. She moved slightly and didn't feel anything restraining her. Would she feel strong enough to free herself from this man? He was big. *You're also big AND strong.* She felt bolder. She would wait for him to come near. She had to get out of here before he killed her. She had to attack him.

She heard him shuffle close to her and knew she needed to act.

'I am happy you're still sleeping my lovely. The electricity is gone. We have to work quickly. All I am going to do is lift your arm. You will feel just a little twinge as I make the cut. You will love it when your blood gushes to serve Him.'

She resisted stiffening her body as he lifted her right arm and felt the pressure of the knife on her wrist. With all the strength and speed that she could muster, Toks snatched the knife from him and heaved away from the block. Her legs felt leaden as she hobbled to the corner of the room. Her breath came fast and heavy and she could hear nothing else. He seemed to have moved faster than her. She felt a huge pressure on her back as he jumped on her and they crashed to the concrete floor. She felt the crunch of her left arm and knew something had broken. She screamed in agony but refused to let go of the knife. He violently rolled her over and with a mad scream of pain and rage Toks lifted the knife and blindly stabbed upwards. There was a loud groan and he collapsed on top of her. She felt a gush of warm blood wetting her top. With the little strength left in her, she rolled him off her body and collapsed back on the floor. The movement seared her brain with pain and she sank into a peaceful darkness.

***

Philip had a warrant to search Esme's flat. Heads popped out of doors as neighbours stared at the swarm of police officers.

Philip directed them.

'We are looking for evidence of the pots, and anything that will tie her to the rituals. A key to the bunker is the most important. Let's spread out and search every area. Time is running out fast!'

They fanned out and Philip stood thinking, then walked around looking at the ceiling. If there was a loft then they needed to find it. He walked back into the tiny hallway and saw the trap door in the ceiling. 'We need a ladder!' he shouted.

Kingsley, a bulky officer of African Caribbean descent whom Philip knew to be reliable, brought a short ladder. 'I found this in the kitchen,' he said.

He looked at Philip. 'I can go up and check.'

'I'll go,' said Philip, and climbed the short ladder, pushing in the trap door. The smell that hit both of them made Kingsley shout out. More uniforms came running. Philip pulled himself in and closed his eyes to get used to the dark. He searched for a light switch but could not locate one. He walked carefully and flicked on a small torch light he took from his pocket. There was no doubt that there was something dead here. The loft was large as he moved cautiously forward. He realised Kingsley had also joined him, along with a younger looking officer. They fanned out and Philip saw the pots first. There were about six grouped in a semicircle. He looked in the first one. Empty. They were all empty.

He walked into the far corner of the room and the smell was stronger here. There was a large cage structure and curled in a corner was a small, still, human form. They both scrabbled to the cage and Philip unlatched it and crawled in. He could hear Kingsley urgently calling for an ambulance. He turned the body over and shone the light over the face. It was a young girl, unconscious. Venus! It had to be. He felt her pulse but it was very faint. He carried her out. She weighed nothing – light as a feather. Esme had locked her in a cage like an animal. He could smell excrement and urine, and still that stench of death. He carried her and carefully climbed down the ladder.

How long would it take the Paramedics to arrive? He laid her down on Esme's couch and remembered with sadness that this little girl would have been upstairs when he had come to question Esme. Her eyelids fluttered but did not open. Someone brought water and he wet her dried, chapped lips. The ambulance siren was deafening and he heard heavy boots running up the stairs. When they entered he reluctantly let go.

Kingsley came up to them.

'Sir, you need to come back up.' Philip looked at his serious face and nodded. They crawled up the ladder and Kingsley pointed up to the ceiling. Philip saw it. Suspended above them was a kind of drum, almost resembling a beer cask. The thick rope that held it up snaked to the other side of the loft. They walked to a wheel contraption with a handle and Philip realised this would have been built by Steve Briggs and definitely assisted by Esme James. He turned the handle and slowly let the drum down. The smell got stronger and he prepared himself. When it touched the ground, they crowded round it and viewed the horrific remains. Poor little Grace's torso.

Philip brought out his phone and called Katherine.

'We've found what we're looking for in Esme's loft. The missing girl, Venus, in a cage. The torso, the pots...' he said. He looked around. Someone had finally found the light switch. The space reminded him of Emily's room when she was deep in her relationship with Austin. It had been converted to a sort of shrine, with figurines of African female deities dotted around. There were batik materials of white and red. Cowrie shells scattered around the base of the pots. This was going to be a big job for SOCO. He ordered everyone to go back down. They had to leave in order not to further contaminate the crime scene.

Within half an hour Philip was back at the Hopper residence. His phone rang. It was the station.

'Hello sir, it's duty Sergeant Henry. John Hopper is asking to speak to you. I thought it might be important. Will you come to see him?'

'There's no time. Put him on.'

John Hopper's voice came over the line soft and shaky. 'Detective Dean?'

'Yes.'

'I cannot excuse what we allowed in our home. We should have stood up to Stevie more. We should have. But I think I know the code to the vault. Stevie was obsessed with his mother, who was abusive and a drug addict. She died 2 years ago and knowing him he might have used the date of her death. Try 100712. That's all I can think of.'

'Thank you,' said Philip as he ran into the house. Uniforms ran after him as he flew down the basement to the vault. He keyed in the code and the door clicked open, just like that.

They crept in silently and Philip tried to make things out in the darkness. They could not afford to flash their torches till they found Toks. He made out two shapes on the ground in the far corner of the small cubic room. Toks, huddled, awake and blankly staring at the bulk on the floor. Philip shone his torch.

'Toks?'

She looked up with a strained smile and tried to stand up. He ran to her and nearly slipped on the wet floor. Lights suddenly flooded the room and he realised that it was Steve Brigg's blood. He was on his side with wide staring eyes. Philip knew he was dead, even as the officers started CPR.

He sat beside Toks. Her left arm was at an odd angle and he could see bone sticking out through her top that was red with blood.

'You'll be ok.'

She tried to nod and gasped with pain.

Paramedics entered the now crowded space and set to work on Steve. Two of them came to Toks and, having secured the injured arm, gently lifted her onto a stretcher. Philip knew she had lost a lot of blood from the injury, but at least she was alive. He looked at the raised concrete block. Stevie had been close to butchering her like a sacrificial animal. He left officers to search the lair while he followed Tok's ambulance to the hospital. Tok's son, and a man whom he took to be his dad, were already in the waiting area. He had called them on his way. He looked at Bode's red-rimmed eyes. He was sitting very close to his father.

The boy approached him.

'Is my mum okay?'

The father stretched his hand to Philip.

'I'm Femi, Bode's dad.'

'I'm Detective Dean, Tok's partner.' Philip shook his hand and looked at Bode again. He had noticed him clenching his hand. 'What's happened to my mum?' the boy asked in a choked voice.

'I'm sorry. We were following an investigation when she was held hostage.'

Femi, looking shocked, placed his hand on his son's shoulder.

They all sat in silence and waited. Much later, a doctor entered the room and they jumped up. He looked at everyone and nodded his acknowledgement to Philip, who had earlier introduced himself.

'She sustained two fractures on her left arm and lost a lot of blood but is stable. She needs to rest.'

***

Coretta's eyes filled with tears as she listened to Richard.

'It was horrendous what she went through. It was all over the news.'

They were lying close together in bed. She had her head on his chest. 'I'm so glad we'll be home before too long. I must see her. Poor Toks. This was her first case as a detective.' Then she turned and looked at him. 'Richard?'

'Hmm?' His mouth was on her head as he held her even closer.

'What if I said that I found a child we could adopt?'

She felt his body tense. Her mind went back to the orphanage. She had wasted no time in telling Melissa about it. Her sister, with her influence, had made some phone calls.

'Don't expect too much, Coretta,' Melissa had said. 'This is Nigeria. Hopefully they will get together and sort the place out. It'll be hard for them to even track the children's families unless mothers come forward. There are many more orphanages like that. We will do something to help, but those children already gone are gone I'm afraid.'

Coretta looked at her sister to gauge her reaction when she said. 'There was a child there….'

She saw Melissa's eyes widen. 'You mean…?'

'I would like to find out more about her. I just felt right with her.' She had looked away from Melissa. 'Me and Richard could try and have her.' She felt her sister's arm around her shoulder.

292

'Do you want me to find out?'

'Yes, please.'

'I will, but you have to talk to Richard,' said Melissa.

'What about the child?' Richard asked now, quietly.

'You need to see her to understand.'

She felt his arms around her as he held her tight. 'Are we sure about this?'

'Just wait till you see her.'

'How do we do that? We're off tomorrow.'

'We can postpone the flight one or two days.'

She turned and looked at him. His eyes looked wet. He held her face and looked deeply into hers.

'I'm sorry about how I've been in the past,' she said. 'Very selfish.' She pushed into his arms as he held her closer. She would be glad to slow down on the job.

***

DSupt Amos was briefing the team. 'Thanks to a great team, most especially DS Philip, DC Ade and DS Bates, Steve Briggs is dead. Killed by DC Toks in self-defence. She escaped with a badly broken arm and will be fine. The doctors had been afraid of blood clot, but that danger has passed.'

Philip tuned him out as he thought about all the outcomes.

Venus was recovering in hospital. That would take a while. She had been starved and caged like an animal.

Esme James was awaiting trial without bail. There was enough evidence at her home to send her to jail for the rest of her life. She had not only been part of the killing of Grace, but had helped to distribute her body parts to the parks. She was also a private tutor and made her money that way. She used to teach Venus and her friend Teresa. Venus must have met her near the estate and she lured the girl away. Venus would have had no fear as it was her private tutor.

They pieced the rest together. Esme travelled everywhere to tutor and received cash. She had been the one that dropped Grace's severed hand by the block of flats. She had done it as what she called a first free offering to the Orishas. There was no connection to the torso in the Thames. She and Steve Briggs were too young anyway. They had bought Grace from Margaret. Philip hung his head. To imagine that children were still bought and sold in the Britain of twenty-first century!

Esme had been the one to befriend Margaret at the hospital where the woman worked, when she attended as an outpatient the year before as a mental health patient. It was why she stopped teaching.

The briefing was over. Superintendent Amos inclined his head to Philip and he went to him. DCI Jackson joined them.

'Good work, Dean.'

'Thank you,' he said, and made to leave both men.

Superintendent Amos stopped him and gazed at him steadily. 'Dean, you have made your feelings known of what you think of the force. You have an admirable record and I would once more like to recommend you for Inspector. You're long overdue.'

Philip saw Jackson nodding vigorously.

'I would like to think about it,' he said.

'You still have to follow procedure for it but you are more than able to,' said Amos.

'Thank you,' he said, and left them.

Forty

Toks was finally back home from hospital and now watched Philip as he sat uncomfortably on one of her chairs in the front room. Bode had disappeared after he had made Philip his cup of coffee. Femi had just left the house. She did not want to dwell in that direction. Surely the man had business to do elsewhere, yet he insisted on staying and looking after her. Thankfully her parents would be arriving soon.

'And how are you now?' asked Philip.

Shitty, crappy and sore. 'Very well. I'm much better now.' Except for the terrible nightmares waking her up in the middle of the night, drenched in sweat and shaking with terror. *He's still out there.* She looked at Philip and knew he could read a bit of her thoughts. Briggs was dead. She killed him.

'Do you believe that… there's evil?' she asked. She wasn't sure why she asked. Did she care if he believed in evil or not? 'Sometimes, I do,' he said, and she saw a slight shake of his right hand. He casually put it in his pocket but she had seen it. She was getting to know how to read Philip Dean. Maybe he was starting to believe a bit more. He would not like that.

'Do you know, I tried to find out about people like him on the web,' Toks said. 'They're like familiars, absorbing dark powers and using it for evil means. I don't think Esme James or even the Hoppers had a chance.'

Toks saw that he seemed to be struggling with something that he wanted to say and smiled to encourage him – a smile was the last thing on her mind, but she gave him one anyway. He seemed to make up his mind then and looked her straight in the eyes.

'You will be going through a formal debrief once you're better, but I'd like to ask, how did you feel?' His face turned red as she had never seen it before and she almost felt his pain.

'Feel?' she asked, puzzled.

He cleared his throat and then coughed. 'Your faith, I mean. Steve Briggs might have killed you. I deeply regret that we didn't rescue you earlier.'

'No, need. It was my fault for not telling you.'

He stared at her. 'We will discuss that another time.'

'In answer to your question, I was terrified,' she said quietly as her mind travelled back to the steel vault. 'I honestly thought I would die.'

'But you didn't,' he said quietly. 'Did you still believe in God? In the fact that you could still live?'

Tok's mind cleared and she understood his discomfiture. She was silent for a while and then truthfully answered. 'I did not think that I would live. At the same time, I was comforted by the scriptures of the bible and by singing praise. I felt deep warmth and reverence even then—perhaps that is where my last strength came from.'

He nodded and said, 'The knife was buried deep into him, to the hilt. Did he fall on it?'

She shook her head, remembering. 'No, I drove it into him.'

She stopped, suddenly tired. It was time for her to go lie down. He seemed to sense this and stood up.

'Take good care of yourself, Toks.'

'Thanks.'

She watched him walk out and let her head loll back on the chair.

Acknowledgments

In remembrance of 'Adam'
(The torso of the boy found in the Thames, 2001) and other
unknown 'Adams'.

Thanks to the following people;

For my children and family, who continued to cheer me on.

Kadija George, for believing in me over more years that I can
count.

Irenosen Okojie, for being a champion.

My editor, Cherise Lopes-Baker, who sweetly guided me to
the finish.

Jacaranda Books, for picking me as part of their bold twenty
black authors in 2020 initiative.

SI Leeds Literary Prize for creating a prize for Black and Asian
women. *Deadly Sacrifice* would have stayed in the drawer
without this.

Special mention to my Crime Writers of Color family. I am blessed to be in the midst of the greatest writers of color in the world.

About the Author

Stella was born in London, brought up in Nigeria and lives in London. She works as a Business Intelligence Analyst. Stella is a cake enthusiast and an avid foodie who writes about Food, Culture and Tech on her blog africanbritishness (https://africanbritishness.com)and on Medium. Her dream is to travel around the world to taste and experience food from different cultures. Stella believes that her experience of growing within two worlds has given her a unique perspective. *Deadly Sacrifice* was shortlisted for the SI Leeds Literary Prize 2016.

Her website: https://stellaonithewriter.com
twitter @sonithewriter,
Instagram @stellaonithewriter
Facebook: @sonithewriter